Other books by Annie Russell:

The Changeling : A New Orleans Faerie Tale
(The Faerie Tale Chronicles – Book One)

The Journey Stone : A Charlevoix Faerie Tale
(The Faerie Tale Chronicles – Book Two)

Of Ghosties and Ghoulies: A Handbook Of
Things That Go Bump In The Night.

Contributing Author to:

Brigid's Light: Tending the Ancestral Flame of
the Beloved Celtic Goddess
(Available from Weiser Books)

Acknowledgments

I am indebted to the following people and organizations who have been invaluable during the research and writing of The Mirror Dance.

My editor, **Emory Elgar**, for her eagle-eye, love of language, and all-round good humor. I can't thank her enough for coming along on this journey with me through the land of Faerie Tales.

Jack Russell, Jr.'s incredibly intuitive artwork.

The New Orleans Historical Society

Karen Lynne and **Dawn** for reading snippets, as well as sending valuable insights and suggestions.

Georgetown University's The Berkley Center for Religion, Peace, and World Affairs

My Husband for his never-ending support.

For the real Vera -

Thank you.

The Mirror Dance

A French Quarter Faerie Tale

First hardcover edition November 2022

Edited by Emory Elgar
Layout by Jack Russell Jr.

ISBN 978-0-578-38173-2 (Hardcover)
ISBN 978-0-578-38174-9 (Paperback)

NoMi Press
annierussell.net

Chapter 1

Late Spring, Ireland (1876)

The young girl ran up the narrow dirt path as the sun sent its first weak rays over the horizon. The tall grasses leaning over the way hung heavy with early morning dew that left her shoes and stockings sodden. Tomorrow would be La'Bealtaine and there was much to get ready before then. Despite the discomfort from her wet feet and legs, she pushed on, looking forward to warming her toes by the stone hearth in the kitchen.

Turning the sharp bend that signaled the end of the meadow's path and the beginning of the manicured grounds of the manor, the smells and sounds of the great house drifted over her, carried on the early morning breezes—fresh bread baking in the rounded stone ovens and the sharp tang of early Gairleog Mhuire, or Crow Garlic, gathered to flavor soups and other savories for the festival. The lowing of cows ready to be milked sounded a counter note against the sharp tones of the geese as they made their rounds about the packed dirt of the courtyard. The cook's guttural rebuke to a small child and the slapping sound as one large meaty hand met one bony buttock caused the running girl to pick up her pace. The girl had been on the receiving end of that hand more times than she cared to remember and wanted not at all to add another incident to the list.

As she ran past, a cantankerous flock of geese scattered, ensuring that a secretive entrance was no longer possible. She hoped that she wasn't terribly late. As she rounded the final corner and slid into the kitchen, the recent recipient of the cook's ire skirted past her, his tears leaving clear tracks down the otherwise dirt-caked skin of his cheeks.

"'Tis time ye made it," came the gruff voice of the cook who was bent over a large kettle of pottage, her ample behind obscuring most of the hearth.

"The lady would have ye attend her. Wipe yer face and put on a clean apron then be about it—I'll not be in trouble for yer laziness."

Mary kept her eyes down as she slipped on a clean apron and used her own soiled one to wipe her shoes and stockings, only managing to smear the mud more evenly rather than wipe it clean away. Being summoned by the mistress of the house was neither an honor nor a privilege, and she could feel her heart beating against her ribs like a trapped and terrified bird. She stood up and, seeing that there would be no words of comfort—or otherwise—from the cook who was more inclined to cover her large behind than protect the younger workers in her charge, Mary left the warmth of the kitchen and crossed the courtyard to the main house.

As a day worker, Mary was not afforded the luxury of servant status and was therefore not provided a room or a cot. She was paid in seasonal produce and a small amount of meat that she brought back to her family's cottage which added much-needed sustenance to their meager holdings. Her father and brothers worked the fields and pastures of the manor house in exchange for the rent of the land on which their home sat, while her mother and younger sisters tended to the small kitchen garden, and livestock. Their dairy cow was allowed to graze on the manor's ridge with the other tenant's cows and was driven back every evening by the young boy who lived a field over to the west, his cajoling and cursing signaled the end of the small group of cottages' workdays as regularly as any clock. Mary was sent to the Big House as a day worker in the hopes of being hired as a servant, a position seen as a step above and out of the cottage. Once exposed to the practices and patterns of the higher classes, Maggie O'Neil hoped for a better life for her daughter. The owners of the Big House were middling, at best, on the county's social ladder—although, that meant nothing to the thoughtful and ambitious woman on the bottom-most rung. Even a rung or two up was better than the bottom as far as she was concerned.

The haughty housekeeper stood at the ready, holding the heavy wooden door open as she stepped into the dim interior of the hall. Following the imposing figure, Mary walked quickly over the uneven fieldstone and tried not to slip on the unfamiliar flooring as she was used to the soft, pounded earth strewn with rushes and grasses. Her toes caught on jutting edges of the crudely formed stones and her footfalls echoed from the floors, bouncing off limed walls and carved mouldings. Despite all the manor house's artistic improvements over her family's one-room cottage, Mary found it cold and inhospitable.

The housekeeper stepped aside and pushed the skinny dark-haired girl through a heavy tapestry that hung from the beams of the ceiling, sectioning one space within the large room from another. As the curtain fell closed, the woman made a quick sign of the cross, a ritual that would brand her a Papist in this Protestant household and spell her immediate banishment—if not imprisonment—if it were seen by her employers.

As Mary's eyes adjusted to the sudden gloom, she heard hooves on stone and wondered why the Big House would have animals within, a practice common to the poorer cottages but unheard of in the higher classes.

"My lady?" whispered Mary into the semi-darkness, trying desperately to make out the type of animal that was in the alcove with them. There was no scent of cow or sheep, only the sharp tang of medicinal herbs and plants that made up her mistress's toilet.

"Mary O'Neil. Thank you for attending me," came her mistress's Scottish brogue from deep within the shadows. The clip-clop of hooves on stone had ceased.

"Of course, my lady," whispered Mary, dropping a curtsy despite the lack of light. If her mistress would see her and note the lack of respect, a thrashing would certainly follow. Though, given the lady's known volatile temperament, a thrashing or tongue lashing could happen anyway. Aisla MacDuffee was well known in the region for her unpredictable nature and her Scottish Highlander roots, one contributing to the other in equal measure as far as the local Irish peasantry was concerned.

A candle flared as flame was set to wick, and Aisla MacDuffee's burnished copper hair that framed her pale skin emerged from the shadows. Mary had never seen her mistress, but her visage had been described in detail from cottage to cottage with lurid stories detailing how her skin stayed line-free and so smooth. Mary had little use for stories and assumed that the woman's perfect skin was a lucky happenstance of not having to work the fields or be subjected to the summer sun's rays.

Dipping another curtsy to be on the safe side and keeping her eyes positioned down, yet not so far down as to not be able to peek at the woman who summoned her, Mary waited for her instructions. Her heart still tripped painfully within her chest, and she would be very glad to be done here, returning to her kitchen duties where the dangers were known and easily avoided.

"Please come in. I've set tea," purred Aisla as she lit two more candles from the first and placed them on the ledges that surrounded the small space.

Mary bobbed her head and moved further into the room expecting that she was being tested in the laying of the tea accoutrements for further work in the Big House. How proud her mother would be! Lifting her head to better see what was being asked of her, Mary stopped in surprise. The scrubbed wooden table was already set with cups, saucers, a teapot, and a small jar of honey. Scones were laid out on a platter with cream and jam to the side of that. It was lovely and smelled wonderful. Most importantly, it was complete and therefore Mary had no idea what was expected of her.

"My lady?" she said to the woman who sat watching her, a sly smile playing on her lips.

"Please sit, Mary," she instructed as she stood and, walking around the small table, pulled a chair out and motioned for the dumbstruck girl to sit.

Because doing as she was told was second nature to her, Mary walked to the proffered chair and sat down. She felt like she might be sick, surely this was not right. A thin white arm reached over her shoulder and poured the fragrant tea into the small cup and added a drop of honey to it. Next, a scone with jam was placed on the delicate plate in front of her.

Aisla's voice purred from behind, "The jam is from our own hedgerow's berries and is simply delicious. Please try some."

Again, despite her growing fear, Mary did as she was told and took a bite of the scone. At any other time, it might have been delightful, but for the terrified child stuck in this ghastly tea party its sweetness was cloying and the pastry dry as dust. She sipped her tea to help swallow the crumbs stuck in her throat when a sharp burning along her neck caused her to jump and spill the hot liquid onto her clean apron.

"Ssshhhh, my dear. Ssshhhh," whispered the redhead as she took the delicate teacup from Mary's hand and wrapped one bare alabaster arm around the girl's thin shoulders. With the other hand, Aisla pushed Mary's head to the side, her right ear almost touching her right shoulder, and exposed her neck. The pain grew stronger as the skin was pulled taught. Frozen like a hare in fear and confusion, Mary could only stare wide-eyed at the flickering candles lined up along the wall as the Lady of the House continued to gouge deep wounds along her neck, bending to lap the beaded blood like a contented house cat with a saucer of cream.

The Fae housed within the exhausted and sickly body of Aisla Drummond MacDuffee found this young and healthy human much more to its liking- so strong, healthy, and vibrantly *alive!* Being so young, this human was not confined yet to marriage or a manor house; the Baobhan Sidhe smiled at the vistas that would be open to it now.

The candles had long since burned down when Mary O'Neil awoke in the darkened chamber — cold, confused, and sore. Lines of fiery pain shot down her neck from her hairline to her collarbone. Disjointed memories of a pale-faced redhead who served her tea and biscuits and the clip-clop of hooves on stone looped over and over in her head and remained fuzzy and unclear no matter how hard she tried to recall the incident with any clarity.

Still shaky, Mary stood carefully and gripped the table's edge for balance. Despite her watery memory of a tea party, of sorts, the table was empty save for a lone candle burned to a nub in its holder.

As she made her way back into the main room and out into the courtyard, Mary was stunned to see that the sun had set and darkness had begun to pool from the corners and edges of the manor house and stables, spilling out into the courtyard like molasses. She made her way across the yard and entered the kitchen where the cook was kneading balls of bread dough—her sleeves pushed up past her elbows, arms the size of hams dusted in flour.

"Ma'am, I—," whispered Mary.

"Yer supper is on the hearth, though I doubt it will be fresh now. Eat it up. You'll need yer strength. Then wash yer bowl and go home; it is late, and I don't want yer Mam yellin' at me that you are out past dark," interrupted the large woman. Her tone was abrupt, devoid of concern, yet somehow knowing.

"What happened?" asked Mary in a small voice.

"Nothing has happened. Nothing. You fell asleep and the mistress was kind enough to let you nap. Eat and go home, now. 'Tis late."

Mary took her bowl from the hearth and removed the linen that draped over it. A pottage of root vegetables and peas with a couple of onion slices for flavoring had congealed within the wooden container. Since the cook was watching to see that she ate, she spooned the mass of mushy vegetables and starches into her mouth and swallowed quickly, praying that it would stay down. While she still felt shaky and weak, her stomach was rebelling at the thought of food. All she wanted was her bed and her family.

Mary took a dipper of water from next to the breadboard, wiped her mouth, and turned to go.

"Leave the apron; it's the House's," barked the cook. Mary slipped the closest thing to a uniform she had over her head and dropped it beside the table.

The cook watched the skinny child shuffle down the trail away from the manor and took the blood-stained apron and tossed it onto the fire, watching as the flames consumed the only evidence of what had happened to the girl.

"Will this one take?" the cook asked the cat that sat next to the window. "Tomorrow is the great festival and if this one doesn't work, we will be burnin' aprons for the next year, and I'll never be able to go home."

Chapter 2

Maggie O'Neil doused the household fire in the cold predawn hours, her thoughts a jumble of fear and exhaustion. When her daughter failed to come home in time for the evening meal, she assumed that Mary had been held over by the cook to assist in the preparations that would soon consume the Big House; La'Bealtaine was one of the most important festivals and had been since her great grandmother's time and *her* great grandmother's time. The Church could spin it any way it wanted but the rites of spring remained firmly entrenched in the people and the land. When Mary still had not come back with the setting of the sun, Maggie began to worry and sent one of the boys to the manor house's kitchen to fetch her home. However, the lad returned alone and said that the cook had not seen her since the midday meal.

Maggie didn't like nor trust the cook; she was a querulous woman, both mean-spirited and cruel, who was more interested in maintaining her position than the wellbeing of the young people sent to her to work. Removing her soiled apron and smoothing her skirts, Maggie left by way of the narrow trail that first her daughter and then her son had taken earlier that day. The cook may well lie and abuse the younger ones, but that would not be the case with Maggie O'Neil.

As she hurried up the trail the clip-clopping of hooves could be heard approaching and Maggie stopped, curious who would be riding a horse on the narrow footpath. As the sound grew louder, the hairs on Maggie's arms stood up painfully, and chills rolled from the crown of her head to her feet. Something was wrong; something was very, very wrong. The clip-clop of hooves was unmistakable, but the sound supported only two legs, not four.

"Blessed Bride, protect us," whispered the frightened Maggie O'Neil as the sound continued toward her. She stood still and silent as the clip-clop of the hooves rounded the small bend. Holding her breath and whispering prayers and invocations to the Old Gods and the Saints alike, she took a deep breath and raised her eyes to see what was coming up the trail.

"Mam!"

Maggie heard the cry, knew the voice, recognized her daughter, and was yet frozen in place—so strong was her shock.

"Mary! Where have ye been? What has happened?" cried the distraught woman looking over the pale, disheveled figure standing before her. There was nothing about her that suggested danger and nothing on her feet that would make the sound of hooves, yet Maggie's entire body reacted as if a mighty predator stood before her. Her eyes, however, saw only the skinny and pale-faced body of her daughter.

Swallowing her terror and confusion, and wrapping one arm around Mary's thin shoulders, Maggie led her daughter back up the trail to the cottage, her head swimming with half-formed thoughts and ideas.

After gently stripping the muddy woolens from her daughter and putting her to bed, Maggie settled herself by the hearth and stared at the smoke-darkened interior of the stone fireplace. Her eyes unfocused and her vision turned within. Her husband, noticing his wife's faraway gaze, slipped quietly past her and to bed. He had learned long ago that the women of his wife's family line saw and felt many things he could not. Best to leave them to it—if he was needed, he would know soon enough.

As the last wisps of smoke from the smothered fire disappeared up the chimney, Maggie shook her head to clear the fuzziness in her head, born of worry and lack of sleep. No matter what had happened yesterday, and she had a sinking suspicion of what that might be, today was still a festival day and certain observances were required. Maggie checked the room behind her and noted the dark linen draped over the cottage's only mirror and the fireplace, now dark and cold. The boys and her husband had left to help set the bonfires, leaving only Mary sleeping soundly in the small loft overhead. Maggie whispered a prayer that her daughter would continue to sleep until she returned. Taking up the large wicker basket sitting by the door, she left the house and walked through the meadow to meet her own Mam, Bridgette. Together they would gather long rushes and grasses as well as the bright yellow flowers that would adorn their home's windows and doorways. Later, when the sun reached its highest point, the two households would gather their livestock and the prepared bundles of rushes from the meadow. The villagers and their animals would dance between the massive bonfires set along the fields, allowing the smoke to cleanse and bless them. The rushes would be lit from those sacred flames and carried back to the beflowered cottages to relight the household's hearths with the blessed fires of Mayday. Maggie hoped her mother could help her decide what had befallen her daughter during their outing. If it were as she suspected, perhaps her mother would know how to keep the girl safe from what had been unleashed. While the Great Fire Festivals cleansed and blessed, they also had the power to open the way for darker powers to roam. It was this that frightened Maggie to the bone.

Malcolm MacDuffee opened one eye to glare at the sunlight that intruded upon his sleeping chambers. Festival day or no, he felt poorly and would have preferred to stay in bed. The lethargy and weakness that had plagued him for so many months held fast no matter what his wife had the cook concoct for him to imbibe or bathe in.

Rising stiffly, the master of the manor pulled his trousers up over his nightshirt and shrugged into his jacket. Bending over to pull up his stockings caused a wave of weakness and dizziness to wash over him, and he squeezed his eyes shut, waiting for it to pass. It always passed.

Having managed to get dressed without falling over completely, Malcolm shuffled over to the heavy tapestry that separated his sleeping chamber from his wife's. He pulled it aside, thinking to wish her a good morning, and stifled a cry of shock at the sight within. Aisla MacDuffee lay sprawled half on and half off her bed. She was naked, and the bedclothes were bunched around her legs as if she had tried to stand, got tangled, and simply dropped back down onto the feather-filled mattress. While all of this was disturbing enough, it was the condition of her naked body that caused Malcolm to cry out; Aisla's skin, famed for its alabaster perfection, was the color of yellowed parchment with deep lines to match. Her eyes, normally a clear, bright green, were dull and brown. Her teeth, with their gums sunken and receding, appeared sharp and wolf-like. Most disturbing, however, was the mess from a dark, soil-like substance that ran from her mouth and down between her breasts as if she had vomited the earth itself.

Upon hearing the cries of fear and dismay from the master, the housekeeper rushed in and stopped suddenly in front of the morbid scene.

"Go! Get the cook!" cried Malcolm.

The stunned housekeeper fled across the small, packed dirt yard to the kitchen, more than happy to lay the whole situation at the cook's feet. The large, flour-dusted woman seemed to take the franticly described scene in stride and left the traumatized housekeeper alone by the cold and fireless kitchen hearth.

Scattering clacking geese in her wake, the cook entered the Big House and strode purposely into the sleeping chambers of her master and mistress. She stepped silently past the stunned Malcolm, moved past the body of Aisla, and opened the wooden trunk that sat next to the bed. She knelt and pulled through piles of dresses, mantles, and aprons until she located a small wooden box set with metal corners and a hinged lock. She removed a key from within a tall leather boot under the bedstead. Without speaking a word or directing a glance at the master, the cook unlocked the box and carefully spooned a bit of the earth-like vomit from her mistress's chest then closed and re-locked the box. The large woman strode past her master and left the Big House by way of the narrow foot trail that wound its way through the meadow, now filled with villagers busy collecting flowers and rushes for the festival.

As the sun rose above the roof of the small cottage at the end of the lane, the cook slipped inside, heaved her bulk up to the tiny sleeping loft, and slipped the box and its key under the bedclothes of Mary O'Neil.

Chapter 3

Mary woke to the scents and sounds of the fire crackling away just below her sleeping loft. Her family had returned from the festival and had set the household hearth alight with the flames brought back from the sacred bonfires. The smell permeated the small space, wafting from the cottage's fireplace and her family's clothing, heavy and dense with the purifying smoke of the La'Bealtaine flames.

Rolling over to avoid the harsh light of the May sun, Mary's leg bumped against the box that had been left there as she slept. While her memories of the previous day were foggy at best, she was almost positive that she had not brought a box home with her. In fact, at just shy of fourteen years old, she wasn't old enough to own much of anything—let alone a lock box. So where had it come from? Having extricated the box from the tangle of bedclothes, she held it over her head, turning it and noting the decorative metal corners, the large keyhole, and the smooth, stone-like feel of the old wood.

Mary stood up as quietly as possible, not yet ready to face her family and the inevitable questions that she had no clear answers to and held the box up to the window. It was about the size of the round loaves of her mother's bread but squared. The lid was deep and allowed for extra space within. When she tried to open it, she found it to be locked. Shaking the box only resulted in a muffled bumping of whatever was inside.

Mary set the box on the bed and ran her hands under the blankets—hoping that however the box had arrived, the key had made the journey with it. After several passes, her fingers brushed against cold metal and closed around the top of a perfectly nondescript key that could have fit any cupboard in their cottage.

Bending over the box, she carefully inserted the key into the lock and twisted it. The whispering sound of the tumblers moving signaled that it was the correct key, and she held her breath. A few moments too late, she wondered if she should open it. What if it had been stolen from the Big House and left with her to implicate her in something? After all, she couldn't remember much of anything from yesterday, only that she had found her mother on the trail and had been brought home.

"Might as well," she whispered to herself as she carefully lifted the lid.

Mary wasn't sure what she expected but it wasn't this. Inside the box were a few rocks, a small amount of soil, and some dried heather blossoms. Puzzled, she gently shook the box to move around the contents. She thought, maybe upon closer inspection, she would find a necklace, a ring, or a treasure map inside. But no, there were only rocks, dirt, and a few dead flowers. And yet, Mary felt the stirrings of unease about the box and its contents, not to mention its mysterious arrival. She carefully closed the lid, turned the key in the lock to secure it, and hid the box behind the bags of vegetables stored next to her cot— the price of privacy was making do with a loft that held the family's foodstuffs.

The young girl smoothed her blankets, righted her clothing, dropped the key into her pocket, and ran her fingers through her hair. Her family would have questions, and she was unsure how to answer them. She was certain, however, that the box and its contents should remain a secret.

Her family's chatter slowed and stopped as Mary descended the ladder to join them for the last part of the festival's activities. Her brothers, father, mother, and grandmother were gathered around the table enjoying the nettle soup, ale, and sweets that were as much a part of the festival as the bonfires. Mary noticed wound balls of bright ribbon piled next to the door ready for the Maypole dance that would happen after the midday meal. In years past, Mary was the first to the fires, the last one home, and the first back out again to the dances. This year, she saw the celebrations through smudged and foggy eyes. Had she grown too old to enjoy the festival? Was she exhausted with her duties at the Big House? While those reasons made sense, she suspected something else was at play, and it frightened her.

"Weeeellll! Look who's decided to come to the party!" roared her father, flush with alcohol and the heat of the hearth's flames.

"I'm sorry," replied Mary, eyes downcast.

Her father was a good provider and didn't beat his children unfairly, but he was loud and boisterous and made Mary feel timid and ill at ease.

"Collin, leave the girl be," ordered Maggie over her shoulder as she ladled soup into a small bowl.

"Sit," she commanded and set a place for her daughter. Adding a small cup of the yeasty beer, she motioned for Mary who dutifully took her chair.

Maggie and her mother Bridgette exchanged a charged glance, and Bridgette gave a small nod. Maggie stood, patted her daughter on the shoulder as she passed, and walked to the linen-draped mirror. As nonchalantly as possible, Maggie removed the dark material, folded it, and set it aside. The mirror reflected the small family and the bright May day outside the window.

"Mam! Why are ye taking that down? The sun's not set, and the Good Folk will surely find us to play their tricks!" one of the boys shouted.

"Ah, no. We've made all the offerings and followed all of the rules for the eve and today. I imagine we're safe enough from the Fair Folk, my boy," said Maggie to her son as she used the linen to wash the mirror with the tincture that would provide the knowledge she sought. Though, to her son, it seemed as if she were only wiping the dust from the glass.

As Maggie fiddled with the cloth, she stole glances into the mirror at the homely tableau within its frame.

At first, nothing seemed to be amiss. Maggie thought that maybe her imagination had run away with her; there was nothing wrong with her daughter save for being overworked at the manor. She caught Bridgette's eye and shook her head indicating that the mirror displayed nothing of concern. She saw Bridgette take a deep breath and felt her relief flow across the room. Festival days were precarious enough without the possibility of a family member in danger.

And then it happened. Such a small accident, one that should have had no consequence or bearing on the day, and yet it changed everything.

Busy chattering away to his son, Collin O'Neil cut his thumb while attempting to spread the butter onto his bread. It was only a small cut, really, nothing that a quick press of cloth wouldn't fix. But there was blood. Not much, but enough.

As Maggie watched in horror through the mirror's glass, her husband cursed under his breath as two small beads of blood appeared on his thumb. At the sight of the blood, her beloved daughter's eyes rolled back and her head lolled to one side then snapped up suddenly. Her formerly brown eyes were as green as glass and wickedly slanted like a cat's. Her dark brown hair sparked and sparkled with a vibrant red hue as bright as a candle flame. The freckles along her nose faded away as her skin shone a brilliant alabaster white.

Maggie gasped and turned away from the mirror. Mary appeared normal, but there was a sly grin on her lips—a grin too old and too knowing for one so young. Mary was staring at her father's bloodied thumb.

Before Maggie or Bridgette could move, Mary O'Neil launched herself across the table and grabbed her father, dragging his thumb to her mouth where she sucked as much of the blood from it as she could before he threw her off him. Collin gaped in horror, Mary landed in a heap on the stone hearth, and the younger children cried out in terror. Only Maggie and Bridgette stood unmoved and rigid. As much as they wanted it to not be true, Mary O'Neil was not herself any longer.

Chapter 4

Maggie O'Neil held cold cloths soaked in herbs to Mary's face hoping to lessen the bruising and swelling. One eye would likely close shut, such was the damage, and at least two teeth were broken from the walloping her father had meted out, but there was nothing to be done for it. Truth be told, if Bridgette had not thrown herself across the unconscious body of her granddaughter, Collin O'Neil may very well have killed Mary for he understood that his daughter was no longer the only one inhabiting her body. Mary and Bridgette also knew this, but violence came a bit harder for the women who preferred a healing approach.

As Maggie applied cold compresses and poultices to the girl's ruined face, Bridgette flipped rapidly through the small, cloth-covered book that was their most treasured and valuable possession. Ostensibly, the small ledger held household recipes and instructions such as the best time to churn butter, how to make a pie crust, and teas for cough, stomach pains, and the morbid sore throat. While the book did hold quite a few of these entries, scattered here and there—among the best month to plant potatoes and the amount of thyme to add to a cut of lamb—there were other, more secret bits of advice. Next to a recipe for shortbread was a small entry instructing the reader how to tell the most likely outcome of an event by staring into a black-bottomed bowl filled with water. Several pages later, after a lengthy article on repairing pots and kettles, was advice and admonishments on the appropriate offerings to the Fae when a newborn was in the house.

There were recipes for teas that allowed one to see fairy circles and tinctures to wash the eyes of those afflicted with false visions. Along with the names and uses of herbs in household medicine were smaller lists giving the details of herbs that would deter or repel wandering spirits.

As a young girl, Bridgette Kelly had been employed as a servant to an educated woman from England, and it was this woman who had begun the small book as a keepsake for when Bridgette would marry and keep her own house. She taught the young Bridgette to read and write using the book's recipes by having her add to it daily. Bridgette and her mistress added recipes for jam, instructions for cleaning the floors, how to dip candles, and how to break the bones of a hare before adding it to the pie so that the marrow would flavor the dish. As the woman grew older, she began to dictate to her young servant girl the other instructions that were sprinkled throughout the book. Having no daughter of her own, the English woman chose to pass her knowledge to Bridgette. Bridgette asked no questions and obediently wrote what her mistress decreed. On the eve of the full moon—during the coldest March in recent memory—Bridgette was summoned to her mistress's bedside. As she leaned over the old woman to better hear her, birdlike hands fluttered up and out from the bed covers and closed over Bridgette's eyes causing everything to go dark. The old woman whispered a sing-song invocation, dropped her hands, and swallowed a final breath. Bridgette's eyes adjusted, and she found that her world had changed drastically. Colors and light danced around the plants and trees outside the chamber's window. The fire shimmied and shook as if dancing to a tune only it could hear. A miniature man with the dark wings of a beetle folded upon his back ran squeaking across the floor, chased by a mouse that muttered curses in the accent of the English gentry.

Bridgette forced her attention back to her mistress who lay peacefully as if only sleeping. Next to the candle on her bedside table was a note for her adopted daughter that detailed the new power passed to her. The note included how to use this power, how to shut it off to rest, and how to pass it along to her daughter—for it must only be passed from woman to woman, mother to daughter, whether of the blood or the heart.

Bridgette went on to marry a man who died shortly after the birth of their only daughter, Margaret. As her daughter grew in age and intellect, Bridgette taught her to read and write using the blue-leathered book labeled *Faerie Tales* in gold script along its spine. For years, together, they added to it. When Maggie turned fourteen, Bridgette sang the words that would open her daughter's eyes to the Fae. When Maggie married Collin O'Neil, and shortly thereafter had her own daughter, Bridgette whispered the incantation that closed her own, having earned her rest.

"What do you see about the girl?" whispered Bridgette to Maggie, searching the body of her granddaughter for anything amiss. Aside from the bruises and swelling from the beating, she could only see a human child.

"I can see nothing! There is a slight smudge around her, like of soot, but I swear on all that is holy—this is only Mary!" hissed Maggie back to her mother.

"Well, we know that is not true, daughter. You saw the Fae emerge from her in the mirror's reflection and we all saw her suck the blood from her father. It's a wonder the man didn't kill her outright, truly."

Bridgette flipped through the book, muttering and cursing under her breath.

"We know the mirror showed us the truth because of the tincture applied, but what else can it do? Perhaps we can send the Fae back into it?" asked Bridgette, speaking just as much to her daughter as to herself, for she knew the magic that mirrors contained.

"You should rest now, mother. As long as Mary is asleep, we have some time. Collin has agreed to give us a few days before he takes his course. Rest, we'll come back to this," encouraged Maggie.

Nodding, Bridgette stood and set the book onto the bed beside Maggie. She carefully navigated the ladder down into the cottage's main room and left quietly for her own house just down the lane. Her daughter was right; now was the time to rest.

Maggie stared at her daughter, seemingly so small and so young. How had this happened? They had followed all the rules—left their offerings, didn't speak the names, avoided the circles of mushrooms, and in no way offended the Good Folk. These cautionary measures were meant to keep them safe, yet here lay her girl—battered, bruised, missing teeth, and somehow connected to a being not of this realm.

After washing Mary's face once more with the cooling herbal brew, Maggie stood and quietly descended to the cottage's main room.

As she set the soup pot to bubble on the hearth and removed the cover from the bread, Maggie missed two very important events. Despite having the Sight, she was tired, distraught, and therefore too distracted to notice the tall monk standing within the mirror's glass peering out at her. Her exhaustion and the bubbling of the soup obscured the second event; the sound of her daughter walking softly above her head as she gathered her few belongings, the mysterious box, the blue book, and placed them all into the battered suitcase stored next to the potatoes.

46

Chapter 5

Bennette stood within the swirling mists of the In-Between, watching stone-faced as Collin O'Neil beat his daughter to within an inch of her life. With each pounding of the Irishman's meaty fist onto the girl's tender flesh, Bennette grew more and more irate at the injustice of the act. The Unseelie Faerie, the Baobhan Sidhe, had shown itself when Collin had cut himself. The Faerie faded into its young host as soon as the blows began to rain down.

"Coward," muttered Bennette to the Fae, his jaw hard and his eyes narrowed. "Nothing but an opportunistic coward, no better than vermin."

As Bridgette threw herself on top of her unconscious granddaughter to stop the abuse, Bennette stepped back from the glass and into the perpetual twilight that made up the In-Between. The violet mists closed around him as he felt the rough bark of a large oak against his back. He slid down the trunk into a sitting position beneath the soaring canopy of the ancient tree that he had conjured, the energy of the Oak complete within all realms.

With his legs tucked under his plain brown robe, Bennette dreamed of how this journey had begun—at once long ago, into the distant future, and only an hour or so in the past depending on where in the In-Between one chose to stand. Bennette indulged the old comfort of linear time as his memories took him back to the Scotland of his youth—the remote and rocky island off the northwestern coast of the Highlands where he was both destroyed and saved.

Symon watched as his mother bustled about the bedchamber, added a tunic to the trunk, then removed it only to replace it again. He knew that leaving was the best hope he had, not only for a better life but for survival in general, but he wasn't ready to be away from the only home he had ever known—whether he was welcome there or not.

"Hand me those stockings," ordered Alma over her shoulder to her only son.

Symon sat sullen and unhelpful on a chair in the corner of the bedchamber they had shared since his birth a decade previously. While Alma knew that the Abbot would likely confiscate the trunk and its contents upon Symon's arrival, she couldn't, in good conscience, send her only child away with just the clothes on his back. It was heart-breaking enough to send him away at all, but to send him with nothing seemed to add yet another failure to the long list of transgressions that she had racked up in her life thus far.

"I don't want to go," whispered Symon as he handed his mother woolen stockings.

Hearing his voice catch, Alma turned and gathered the boy in her arms. He was small for his age and skinny, physical characteristics that had made his life at the manor more difficult than if he had been able to defend himself against Alfred, the lord's other—and legitimate—son. What had begun as typical boyish tussling had developed over the past year into a dangerous game of cat and mouse as Symon spent his days carefully avoiding Alfred, and Alfred dedicated his time hunting for Symon to deliver increasingly brutal blows with staff, rock, or fist. While Symon tried desperately to evade Albert, Alma more often than not had found herself excluded from the lady's sitting rooms when the other women of the manor gathered for needlework and gossip. Bearing the lord's only other heir proved to be more dangerous than she could have imagined for both her and her son, whether motherhood had been within her control or not. Her gravest mistake had been telling the lady of her husband's assault. How could she have thought of the brute's wife as an ally? How could she have been so naive? But done was done and the consequences of both the attack and her confession were now upon her son, a situation that Alma could not allow to continue. The only recourse left was to send Symon far away, and though it broke her heart, she knew it to be his only chance at survival. So, go he must.

"I know, my love, I know. If there were another way, you must understand that I would do it. But there is not," she crooned into her boy's strawberry blond waves, the result of her mahogany curls and the lord's flaming red hair.

"This is the way that you *live* and then you can *thrive*. You can be so much more there than here. There is nothing for you here but pain, loneliness, and eventual death. You must know that they will not allow you to survive to adulthood within these walls. At the monastery, you will be among the learned where you will be educated. They will protect you there and keep you safe. You must go," she encouraged.

Alma kissed Symon's head, held him firmly by his narrow shoulders, and stood him in front of her. For all his gawkiness, she could see the fine man he would become; tall, thin, elegant in the way of her people, with golden red hair and pale green eyes. She hoped he would be kind, but she did not know if kindness was taught by the monks. Still, she knew it was his only way to salvation and life in this world. The salvation of the next meant little to her, so he must leave her and likely, she would never see him again and that nearly shattered her.

Symon watched as his mother took his measure, her eyes moving up and down his body from the top of his head to the toes of his leather-clad feet. She thumbed the tear from his cheek, kissed the top of his head, and took a deep breath.

"Hand me those other stockings, please, Symon," she requested as if the heart-wrenching speech had never passed her lips and they were only packing his clothes for a short holiday.

Symon did as he was told while admiration for his mother's strength and hatred of her decision fought for space on his pale features. Her strength was unmatched, though. He knew that no matter what, he would be taken to the monastery gates and left there, his new life mapped out with no input or opinion allowed of him.

As Symon and his mother worked in silence, the trunk slowly filled with the boy's belongings, and the shadows lengthened along the chamber's stone floor, signaling the evening's approach.

Alma closed the trunk and latched the lock into place. She summoned a young man to load the heavy box onto the carriage that would take them to the monastery.

Swinging her cloak about her shoulders and pinning it into place, she handed Symon his wrap with a look that suggested additional complaints would not be tolerated. He threw it over his shoulders in a rare display of temper and followed his mother out the chamber doorway, down the spiraling stone steps, and into the pounded dirt courtyard where a cart and horse waited.

"Where is the carriage?" Alma asked the man who was tasked with driving them.

"This is what Herself sent for you," he responded, cheeks reddened from both embarrassment for Alma and the chilled October winds. He had dreaded this chore since it was laid at his feet a day earlier.

"Ah, so it will be like this, will it?" Alma muttered ruefully as she and her son stepped into the cart that had recently been piled high with cabbages for the manor's kitchens.

Alma sat with her back straight and her chin high as if the lowly vegetable cart were the lord's finest carriage. She cast a final look around and ordered the driver to leave.

Symon watched the humiliation of his mother with guilt and anger. His very existence had caused this, and he hated the lord and lady for their casual cruelty. He found himself unexpectedly happy to be leaving this place after all.

Through the gathering evening shadows and then under the bright moon of the early harvest season, Symon and his mother bumped and rolled over uneven cart tracks toward the rocky coast and his new life. As the moon descended into the western sky, the lonely songs of the forest's night birds were replaced by the roaring sea and laughing gulls, and Symon understood that his time with his mother was drawing to a close.

The cart tracks stopped at the end of the world, as far as Symon was concerned. They ran up to the base of a rocky outcropping and stopped—nothing beyond but a long drop into the cold waters of the sea.

The driver ticked his tongue at the tired horse, and the beast came to a grateful stop a dozen yards from the cliff. Without a word, he stepped down from the seat, heaved the heavy trunk from the cart, and dropped it onto the grass beside the path. Symon, clutching his mother in one last embrace, cried for his lost family and life. His desolate cries were carried by the winds and mixed with the raucous laughter of the gulls and the crash of the ocean waves below.

"Go, my son. Never forget that I have loved you more than life itself. Because of that, I will send you to a life that will bring you hope and promise. Make me proud, Symon."

Alma held her only child at arm's length, looked into his eyes, and moved him toward the edge of the cart.

Symon, tears blurring his vision, jumped to the ground and walked to his trunk—it was left sitting in the tall grasses like discarded rubbish.

Wrapping his wool cloak around himself, he sat down and watched as his mother's humble carriage turned around and bumped back along the path the way they had come.

"Symon."

The deep, baritone voice caught him off guard. His heart tripped painfully out of beat within his narrow chest. Spinning around, and almost falling off the wooden trunk on which he sat, Symon saw a tall man, roughly his mother's age, dressed in a finely knit robe tied loosely at the waist with a simple cord. A long hood hung down the man's back, and his feet were clad in quality leather. While the man wore no other ornaments, Symon knew the clothing to be of the highest standard.

"Yes, I'm Symon," he said in a shaky voice that he tried desperately to hide.

"You may come with me," the man instructed.

Symon scrambled up from his makeshift bench, scooted quickly through the tall grasses, and followed the brown-robed man. He imagined someone would be along later to collect his belongings and hoped his mother wouldn't find out that he had left everything he owned sitting on a cliff at the edge of the ocean.

"Where are we going?" he panted as he struggled to keep up with the man's longer stride.

"To the monastery."

"But where is that?" asked Symon, looking frantically around at his surroundings.

He saw nothing but the tall grasses, the cliff, and the wild ocean beyond. He felt desperately frightened and thought perhaps this had been a grave mistake; perhaps this was not a monk but a highwayman who would throw him off the cliff and make off with his trunk.

The monk made no more comments, simply beckoning Symon to follow with the waving of one bell-shaped brown sleeve. Having no other choice, Symon did as he was told.

Just as it seemed that the monk would lead Symon right over the edge of the cliff, the tall man ahead of him made a sharp turn and descended the steep rock face by way of a well-worn, barely noticeable trail that led to the small beach below. Symon could just make out a wooden skiff tied to a scraggly tree that had rooted itself valiantly in the boulders and sand on the shoreline.

"Where is the monastery?" Symon called over the crashing waves.

The monk responded by extending an arm outward with a long finger pointing out to sea.

Symon felt the weight of uncertainty and fear fall heavily upon him; far out at the horizon was the blue-black bump of an island.

"But what of my trunk and my clothing?" he called to his guide. The small wooden boat was only large enough to hold the two of them. There was certainly no room for the carefully packed trunk full of tunics, jackets, and woolen stockings.

"You will be provided with all that you need upon your arrival. *Symon* may have had a trunk of colorful clothing, but *Bennette* will wear a warm robe of the deepest brown and good leather boots to protect his feet."

As the two men reached the beach, they were hit with the full force of the sea's salted gales. Using his arm to protect his eyes from the stinging sands, Symon—now Bennette—stepped into the skiff and sat carefully down at the center of the bench.

"You have been taught to row, I hope," the monk said over the roaring waves.

As the boy scurried off behind the monk, considering his new life as Bennette, Alma sat silent and despondent in the bed of the vegetable cart and wondered what would become of her now. She had succeeded in getting her son safely away from the threat at the manor, but that chore had become her entire life. Now that his safety was assured, she had no idea what she would do with herself. She couldn't very well resume her position as her lady's companion; the arrival of the vegetable cart as her livery was a message in no uncertain terms that she was no longer considered part of the lord's household. And, while not highborn herself, she had been reared and trained as a lady-in-waiting and knew nothing of a servant's work.

Alma started in surprise as the cart came to a sudden stop.

"What is it?" she asked the driver, her tone sharp and alarmed.

"Nothing. Just need to take a minute," came the reply as the young man jumped down from the high seat above the horse and headed toward the wood beyond the trail.

She assumed that the driver needed to relieve himself and felt thankful that he was well-bred enough to walk some ways away rather than do his business right next to where she sat. She resumed her private ruminations, wondering what would become of her now that her goal as a mother was complete.

Alma was so deep in thought that she never noticed the driver come around the other side of the cart; she didn't have a chance to evade his strong arm as it wrapped itself around her neck and dragged her out of the cart. By the time she came to her senses and realized what was happening, it was too late. The sharpened blade approached quickly and sliced her throat, allowing her life's blood to flow out into the grasses that grew between the cart trail and the dark woods.

As her life drained out of her, Alma watched the driver lean over and wipe his blade on the hem of her cloak.

"This is my favorite cloak," she found herself thinking. "I'll never get the stain out."

The sheer madness of that thought forced a laugh from her lips, and blood bubbled from the gaping wound at her neck.

"Run, Symon…. Run…." was the last conscious thought that flowed through Alma's mind as her vision narrowed to a tunnel of branches, partly dead leaves, and the gathering crows above her.

Bennette would never forget his first few weeks on the Isle of Monks, known today as Canna. Despite his valiant attempt at rowing, his skinny arms were simply not up to the task. Halfway across the cold and choppy waters, his escort was forced to take over to avoid their skiff being over-topped by the increasingly large waves. The dark waters and darker skies mirrored his dark and glum mood as he waded through the cold waters of the island's shore to drag the skiff onto the beach. His boots were freezing and sodden as he ran after the monk who offered neither help nor comfort for his small charge's struggles.

The footpath leading to the interior was dotted here and there with tall torches standing as sentinels—cold and unlit in the gathering late-afternoon shadows.

Adjusting his back against his favorite oak tree, safely reminiscing in the In-Between, Bennette wondered if any initial foreboding of the monastery might have been lessened if those torches had been lit. Perhaps it would have been more frightening if the flames had sent dancing, spectral shadows across the unfamiliar land.

Sighing, he closed his eyes and watched his youth play out behind his eyelids. He remembered his small and unadorned room complete with a sturdy cot and heavy woolen blankets, food that was bland but filling, the comforting schedule of masses, prayers, bells, and the candlelit vespers of sundown. The time free of his monastic duties was allotted to education, handicrafts, gardening, and learning the intricate and beautiful art of painting the monastery's books housed within its library. It was soon apparent to everyone at the monastery that Bennette had no great talent in painting, crafting letters, or adding to the illuminated manuscripts, though his reading aptitude was superior to most of the other novices. Where the young man did excel was within the well-kept and tended gardens where the flowers and leaves of vegetables, herbs, and ornamentals thrived and grew tall under his gentle hands and keen eyes.

The years passed for Bennette, and he grew taller, his shoulders widened, and his jaw squared just a bit. He remained long and lithe like his mother's people, but the man he would soon become hid just behind his soft gaze and ready smile. Despite what he believed when he was sent to the Isle of Canna all those years ago, he found himself feeling content, if not somewhat happy, with his life as a monk.

As the purple mists swirled within the place between times, Bennette winced, knowing the memories of her would come no matter what he wished. Like scratching a flea's bite past the point of satisfaction, the sting from remembering still brought a painful joy.

Around his sixteenth year of life, Bennette was sent to the mainland. It had been six years, more or less, since he had come to the isle. It had never occurred to him that he would be sent back among the mainland populace of the Scottish Highlands, but the Abbot decreed it, and Bennette was to leave. Once again, he found that his comings and goings were not under his control. Frustrations bubbled within his breast as he gathered the small number of belongings he had in preparation for his new assignment. The household of John Drummond would send a monthly payment to the monastery in return for a monk to attend to the teaching of its young son.

70

Chapter 6

Bennette opened his eyes and stretched, his fingers brushing the low-hanging branches of the oak tree. The mists danced, and the light remained hazy and lavender. Bennette wondered if the In-Between, a place he considered to be of no-time, was perhaps a place of all-time. When he felt like it, Bennette indulged in philosophical questions about the nature of the In-Between, but he wasn't in the mood right now. Gazing off into the lavender distance, he revisited the moment that changed everything. It was not, as many would believe, his banishment to the Isle of Canna, but rather his return to the mainland of Scotland and introduction to the household of John Drummond.

The young monk understood his assignment and considered how to school a small boy as his carriage traveled over the uneven road leading to the impressive stone house that would be his home for the foreseeable future. His small valise bounced at his feet, and the driver cajoled the tired horse onward, alternating between threatening the poor thing and promising rewards of oats, clean straw, and a comforting rubdown of its heaving flanks.

When the carriage drew up to the gates, Bennette jumped down, preferring to walk the last few feet to the imposing front doors, his legs cramped from the long ride.

Perhaps it was a trick of the sunlight—or maybe his eyes were fatigued from the long trip inland—but, as the doors opened wide to welcome him, Bennette was struck dumb by the beautiful girl who stood there. Her hair was a fiery halo around her freckled face; her eyes blazing in the late afternoon sunshine. She wore a simple tunic over a linen gown and leather shoes that showed her plaid stockings peeking through at the arches of her feet. But it was her smile that left Bennette standing stock-still in the dust, a dozen feet from the girl at the front doors of Drummond House. Then, maybe a cloud moved over the sun, or a tear washed the dust from his eye, but whatever the reason, the halo disappeared. The girl was shoved out of the way by her younger and more robust brother, Peter. Bennette shook his head and squared himself to greet his new charge as the enchanting Aisla disappeared back into the stone house.

Over the months, Bennette settled into the rhythms of Drummond House. John Drummond, widowed and distraught at the loss of his wife and helpmate, was rarely seen around the house. He spent his time riding across the lands that made up his vast estate from early morning until late evening. The cook served John his meals in his private sitting room where he stared into the fire's light until he retired to his bed. Unless it was raining or terribly cold, this was John Drummond's schedule. The servants and townsfolk whispered that his cook was a godsend—a devoted and kind woman who cared for and looked after the melancholy master of Drummond House. Bennette, however, found the large woman cold and somewhat calculating. While he couldn't put his finger on her motivations, he felt they were more self-serving than kind-hearted. However, no one asked the young master's tutor for opinions, so Bennette kept his mouth shut and his eyes open. He and the cook maintained an uneasy acquaintance.

Despite his misgivings about the cook, Bennette found his young charge to be a bright and happy child who was eager to learn and enthusiastic about his subjects. Tutoring Peter was enjoyable, but the highlight of his days came from his young student's sister, Aisla. While not technically his student, Aisla displayed a keen intelligence and often sat in on her brother's studies. It required great concentration for Bennette to keep his attention on his pupil and not on the dazzling young woman sitting next to him.

Many nights were spent in frustrated tears as Bennette's love for Aisla grew along with his knowledge that it was a doomed affair. He was a monk—a penniless one at that—and she was the only daughter of a landed gentleman, destined for marriage with another landed gentleman.

A season passed as Bennette battled with his heart, and Aisla grew more beautiful. The cook's unpleasantness seemed to grow in direct proportion to Aisla's maturity, a mystery not lost on Bennette. The more enchanting the young woman became, the more querulous the older woman grew, and the more uneasy Bennette felt.

Day by day, the sun dropped lower in the sky, the twilight shadows pooled at the edges of the estate's forests, and the winds grew more bracing. The great festival that marked the end of the bright half of the year approached. Soon, the livestock would be driven to slaughter and the bonfires lit. During the gathering darkness, or perhaps because of it, Bennette grew more concerned with the cook's strange behavior and the uninvolved lifestyle of Drummond House's master. John Drummond had had over two years to gather himself after the death of his wife, yet he seemed to only sink further into a world that contained only himself and the cook. The cook, despite her obvious position of favor, grew more hostile toward Bennette and her master's children. The house, at first an agreeable place of employment, became dark and charged with the feeling of undefined danger.

On the night before the great slaughter of the livestock, Bennette found himself wide awake in his small sleeping chamber. The almost-full moon hung high and heavy, and bright yellow light streamed through his window and illuminated the room as if it were midday. Giving up on the possibility of sleep, Bennette slipped his tunic over his nightshirt, gathered his cloak around his shoulders, and slipped his feet into his boots. After straightening his bedding, he left the small room and moved along the darkened hallway from memory rather than sight. The hallway's darkness was thick and far removed from the moon's bright glow.

The great house was still—but not silent— as Bennette made his way to the main floor.

He heard the night watchmen crunching through the drifts of dried leaves that gathered at the edges of the house's exterior, occasionally clearing his throat or belching loudly. Someone moved about in the room to his left that held the master's precious supply of teas, herbs, and spices. Knowing that only John Drummond and his Chamberlain held the key to the space, Bennette slipped past quickly, not wanting to see or engage with either of them.

As he rounded the corner to enter the kitchen, Bennette stopped suddenly to watch the scene playing out in the homely space. The cook had lit a small fire within a stoneware vessel placed on the trestle table which ran the length of the room. The items that were normally scattered across the table's surface were pushed rudely aside, now a jumbled pile of mortars, pestles, wooden spoons, kettles, and linen towels.

Bennette was certain the cook had not noticed him and for that he was grateful for he didn't know how he would explain lurking in the darkened corner if he were caught.

The cook dropped several pinches of dried herbs into the fire, brightening the flames as the plant material burned. The cook muttered and fretted, and Bennette was unsure whether she was singing, praying, or speaking—maybe a bit of each. From the far side of the table, mostly out of his field of vision, she pulled a sheet of parchment toward her. The writing was just visible from where he hid. Holding the parchment over her head, the cook spoke, her words coming faster and faster—her mutterings a chant that set Bennette's teeth on edge and made the hairs on the back of his neck stand on end. The air felt heavy and charged, and the small fire within the stoneware sent its of flames higher, reaching toward the low beamed ceiling. The cook took up a small dirk, secured within her apron's ties, and sliced her thumb where it joined the palm of her hand. She held her hand over the fire and let her blood flow over the flame, hissing and spitting, before she moved her hand over the parchment allowing the red droplets to fall in splattered drops onto the printed words.

Bennette's curiosity was replaced by terror. He turned and made to leave as quickly and as quietly as possible. He had no idea what the cook was trying to achieve, but he knew that whatever her ritual was, it was unlikely to be of a pleasant or holy nature.

Suddenly, a sound coming from the kitchen stopped him cold. Had an animal gotten inside without him being aware? How?

Clip-clop. Clip-clop.

The clacking of hooves echoed against the kitchen's stone floor. The cook's wild chanting had stopped, and even the night watch fell silent. The only sound was that of hooves on stone.

Bennette peered again into the kitchen. The room looked horrifying with wildly flickering flames and a bloodied knife placed on the vellum. The cook stood stock-still, her face frozen and terrified at the creature emerging from the shadows on the other side of the room.

Clip-clop. Clip-clop.

Bennette decided he no longer felt curious about the cook or the events in the kitchen. He wanted very much to be back in his small sleeping chamber, but his feet wouldn't move, and his eyes seemed to be stuck open in horror.

Stepping out from the shadows of the darkened room came a beautiful woman clothed in a dark green velvet gown. Her hair was the burnished red of autumn leaves, her skin as white as the finest porcelain, and her feline eyes were slanted and green like glass. Her generous mouth and berry-red lips smiled cunningly as she moved toward the cook who cowered behind the table where her ritual supplies lay scattered like discarded toys.

Clip-clop. Clip-clop.

"You've called me," declared the Baobhan Sidhe, its voice sounding amused.

"I've gifted you my blood and ask for a favor," stammered the terrified cook.

"A favor?" the Faerie laughed; Its voice bounced off the kitchen's walls, making Bennette's bowels feel watery and loose.

"I wish to be Lady of Drummond House—me alone. Neither of the children shall have the estate. I've written the compact and offered my blood. This I ask of you," the cook replied, her voice stronger but her eyes still staring down at her feet.

"Lady of Drummond House? You?" the Faerie laughed cruelly as it picked up the knife from the vellum and licked the cook's blood from the blade.

"Mmmmm," purred the Faerie as it eyed the terrified woman standing on the other side of the table.

"The compact, though, is *mine* to write — should I choose to offer you the favor that you seek," the creature said slyly, picking up the document from the table and tearing it to pieces.

The cook watched as the pieces floated down to rest, scattered over the table like dirty snowflakes.

"You shall be the Lady of House Drummond but only after I am free."

"Free?" asked the bewildered cook. The ritual hadn't gone to plan, and she did not know how to proceed.

"Bring to me the rightful heir,

She of bright and red-flamed hair.

From her blood will come relief,

And my freedom shall be complete.

Accomplish this as I have asked,

And every detail that is tasked,

And you shall be the Lady true

Of the house that calls to you.

To seal my pact and hold it tight,

Add earth and rock at dead of night.

Place earth within and lock it sound

That part of me may go aground."

Bennette's blood ran cold. The creature was speaking of Aisla! As he watched the nightmare in the kitchen, the Faerie produced an ancient wooden box and handed it across the table to the trembling cook.

"Follow the directions as I've said, and House Drummond will be yours—after I'm free. If you choose not to enter into my contract, I will collect payment from you rather than the girl. The choice is yours. You have a fortnight."

The Baobhan Sidhe melted back into the shadows, and the cook slumped onto the floor, her legs no longer able to hold her. For an unknown amount of time, Bennette watched the flames gutter out and the sun gradually brighten the sky outside.

Chapter 7

Unable to stop the flow of memories, Bennette clenched and unclenched his jaw as the images rushed past, one after the other.

He was certain, that if he were to tell anyone what he had witnessed that night in the kitchen, it would mean his immediate dismissal. He continued to tutor Peter, though he felt it all a sham by then. Aisla, when she joined them, looked pale and weak, her hair less brilliant, her skin dull and yellow. As the days passed, Bennette was painfully aware of the Faerie's deadline. With only two days left until fortnight's end, he could no longer help himself and decided to follow the cook as she brought the evening tea to each family member—the custom after the death of the lady of the house.

Crouching low, Bennette scuttled behind the large woman as she made her way down the main hall. The cook deposited a tray of drinks and sweets into Peter's room, a heartier tray of ale and cheeses into John Drummond's room, and finally a tray of tea and small savory cakes to Aisla. As the woman glided into Aisla's bedroom, Bennette silently placed his foot between the door and the entryway jamb to better observe the room.

Aisla sat on her chair, needlework in her lap, and smiled at the cook as she entered with the refreshments. Aisla motioned to the small table at her side and lowered her eyes to inspect the embroidery. As she squinted at the finely wrought work in the dim light of the evening fire, the cook quickly pushed the tray off the table. The tray, tea, and cakes fell to the floor, and the sharp clattering caused Aisla to prick her finger, startled by the unexpected disturbance. The cook's eyes widened at the sight of the crimson beads on the young girl's thumb, and the woman stepped back into the shadows.

Clip-clop. Clip-clop.

Aisla sat straight and still, every hair on her body standing on end.

Clip-clop. Clip-clop.

The cook watched the shadows at the opposite edge of the room.

Clip-clop. Clip-clop.

Aisla moaned in quiet terror. She knew something awful was about to take place, but her memory had become so foggy lately that she couldn't recall what had happened the previous evenings.

Bennette watched as the beautiful, terrifying creature in a velvet gown emerged from the shadows just as it had almost two weeks ago in the kitchen. The thing—the Fae—that the cook had summoned appeared to be a human, but its feet were deer's hooves, and its features were uncanny.

Clip-clop. Clip-clop. Clip-clop.

The Baobhan Sidhe moved across the room, approaching Aisla as she sat still as a hare and stared straight ahead. Its face radiated sadistic amusement and burning hunger. Delicately, it placed its right hand upon Aisla's hair and tilted her head so that her ear nearly touched her shoulder, exposing her long neck and the almost-healed gouges running from her jawline to her collarbone. Using one long fingernail, the Faerie traced a fresh channel in the girl's neck and smiled as the bloody droplets bloomed along the wound. Aisla closed her eyes as the entity's enchantment worked its way through her mind, and she floated away to a misty place far from the horrors of her bedchamber.

Clapping a hand over his mouth to avoid calling out in anger or fear, Bennette watched as the creature bent and began lapping the blood from the wound on Aisla's neck.

Bennette could watch no more. How long had it been feeding on his beloved Aisla? How many different ruses did the cook have to manufacture in order to draw blood? He didn't know the answers to these questions, but he did know that if Aisla were ever to be safe again, he would need to find out.

Bennette returned to his room that night and packed his few belongings by the watery light of the waning moon. The answers he sought would be most easily found back on the Isle of Canna.

Taking the first horse that looked alert, Bennette made haste to the coast and there to row over the dark waters to the island that would always be his refuge.

Bennette always remembered his homecoming—the warm embraces from his Brothers, the heated water that sluiced the road dust from his exhausted body, and the hearty fish stew that was provided for him before he fell into his bed and slept soundly for the first time in weeks. He slept for a full day and night. He would have slept longer had it not been for the flickering flame of Brother John's candle playing upon his eyelids, teasing them to open and take note of his surroundings.

"You're awake," came the soft voice of the elder monk.

"Aye, it appears I am," replied Bennette.

"Welcome home, my son. You've been away for far too long."

"Thank you, I am very happy to be home," he answered with genuine warmth. He smiled at the older man's gentle, unmistakable greeting.

"When you have dressed and broken your fast, we shall discuss why you've arrived in such a state and ahead of your planned dismissal date. You may find me in the library."

Bennette, in the In-Between, watched the memories of his younger self and wanted to warn him, "Do not go to the library! Do not learn anything more about the happenings at Drummond House! This knowledge comes with a price, and you will be paying dearly for it for so long. Wish your beloved well and walk away while you still can!" But, of course, he could say none of this. Even if he could, he doubted his younger self would have listened.

He continued to watch as his naive and younger self donned his clean robes, slipped his feet into his leather boots, ate his porridge, and went to meet his elder in the library to learn the secrets that would eventually spell his doom.

Secrets such as the Fae and their kind. Knowledge of their ways and what each was. How to avoid them, and, if that was not possible, how to evade them. Details upon details of ancient knowledge that would keep one safe, hidden, or both. How to identify the Courts—the Seelie and Unseelie—of the Fae.

The thing terrorizing Aisla was of the Unseelie Court. It was a creature specific to the Highlands. The Baobhan Sidhe was rare, and they could thank their god for that for it was sly, smart, and cunning. It drank the blood of humans.

As the days passed one into the other, Bennette poured over the old tomes filled with hidden knowledge of those Holy Ones that had lived on the isle before the monks. While the priests had not kept written accounts, the tales had been whispered and kept among the villagers. Eventually, the monks who came after would write them within their huge books disguised as folklore and children's stories. Of course, some of the Brothers still believed the stories to be fiction, but enough of the elders remained to pass the secrets to those with eyes to see and ears to hear so that the warnings and whispers of another race and world that existed just next to our own would remain.

Brother John closed the book with a thud and watched Bennette wrestle with his new knowledge of the Fae, so much learned in such a short time. Truth be told, Bennette had never been considered to receive the ancient knowledge of the Druid priests. Brother John worried that perhaps he was not suitable still, but circumstances demanded the knowledge be passed to him. What Bennette did with the knowledge would be out of the old monk's hands.

"That is the last book we have regarding the Fae and the magics needed to stay safe from them. I cannot stress enough that the safest way is to not engage with them at all."

Bennette tore his eyes from the flickering candle flame and looked at the monk who sat across from him.

"That's not possible, Brother, and you know it. To not engage means that Aisla is lost. She is innocent and cannot simply be left as the Faerie's plaything," Bennette urged.

"What do you plan to do then? Given the lessons you have just received, what would you do to save this young woman?"

Bennette heaved a great sigh and closed his eyes.

"I will return to Drummond House. I will sequester Aisla so the Baobhan Sidhe can no longer feed on her. With its food source gone, it will return from where it came—the forest from which it was summoned."

"And what of the cook? Is she innocent as well?" asked John.

"In my eyes? No. She is not. But in God's eyes? I do not know, and because of that, I will leave the cook to God," Bennette decided.

Brother John felt relieved that the young man would not seek vengeance, though it would be an understandable response. Monks are only human, and humans do things in the name of love that are not always holy. John understood that Bennette loved this young woman with his entire being and accepted this. He could only hope that, with time,

Bennette would move away from this earthly desire and return mind, heart, and soul to the order on the Isle of Canna.

"The journey back is long, and there is little time, son. There is a way that will allow you to travel there and back, but it is fraught with its own dangers. Would you know it and step further into the Mysteries, or would you stay with your current knowledge and return to Drummond House on horseback? The choice is yours. There is no right or wrong choice."

Bennette watched from the violet mists as his young self brashly jumped at the chance to obtain more knowledge and the chance to return to Aisla as fast as possible.

"Fool!" he spat at his own memory and watched as the older monk gave the final instructions that would seal his fate.

Brother John took up the candle and moved to a niche set within the stones of the library wall. From behind a small, painted icon, he removed a miniature scroll secured with a black ribbon.

The young Bennette watched with eager anticipation while the older one, secure within the mists, groaned at the sight.

"Bennette, this scroll contains magic of a high degree and is meant for adepts only. Sadly, you are not one, and you will need to follow the spell very carefully to correctly navigate the world you are about to enter. One misstep, and you will run the risk of being lost between realms. Do you understand?" the monk warned.

"Yes, I understand," Bennette's reply was shaky, and a thin sheen of sweat along his rib cage left him feeling chilled. He suddenly felt unsure.

Brother John pushed the scroll across the table to Bennette.

"Now, read. And read carefully," commanded the elder monk.

The Bennette read the text scratched onto the ancient and yellowed scroll. He read it twice, then three times. Here and there, a word would shimmer and jump, though Bennette was sure that was simply an effect of the candles' flickering flames.

When he finished, Bennette looked up at Brother John, his eyes wide with amazement and fear.

"How many of us know about this?" he asked.

"Within this order, maybe three, perhaps five, of us. And now you," came the reply.

"Is this magic evil? For certain, it is old," whispered Bennette.

"What is magic? Is prayer magic, for isn't a whispered prayer a spell? Is writing magic? When the priests who left us this knowledge had lived, there was no such thing. Magic is a skill. Magic is knowledge. Magic is holy or evil by the intent of the one who uses it. What is your intent, Bennette? Therein lies your answer."

Bennette watched as his teacher stood and pulled aside a tapestry that hung at the far side of the library. The tall, polished bronze mirror shot the candle's flame back at them and illuminated the room. Bennette gasped— a mirror, here! When he read the last of the scroll's Mysteries, he assumed he would have to leave the island to find a mirror.   Yet, here was one cleverly hidden within this library of wonders.

"Be careful and be mindful, Bennette. I hope to see you again soon."

Brother John left the library and his young pupil without looking back. It would do no good for Bennette to see the tears welling in the old man's eyes.

The brash young monk stood before the ancient mirror. What a thing of wonder! Except for wavy reflections in a wash basin or creek, he had never seen a clear reflection of himself, and it felt very strange.

Taking a deep breath, Bennette whispered the words that would allow him to enter the mirror. As he finished the incantation, the mirror's hard metal became loose and as clear as any holy spring's water. He continued his recitations until the purple mists appeared. With a smile, Bennette stepped through the mirror and into the In-Between.

Bennette grew disoriented and panicked. Remembering his lessons, he took a deep breath and imagined a cart path at his feet. His heart slowed slightly when the path appeared as the scroll said it would. Keeping a clear vision of the receiving rooms at Drummond House in his head, for rumor had it there was a fancy glass mirror there, though he had never seen it himself, Bennette walked down his manufactured road toward Aisla.

Standing and stretching his legs, the older Bennette shook his head in disgust, remembering the naivete of his younger self. How much time was wasted walking down a road that didn't exist? Some? None? Weeks? Who knows? What he knew now was that when he stepped through the glass in Drummond House, he was too late. Aisla has been promised in marriage to a wealthy man in Ireland. At first, Bennette thought the marriage meant she was safe from the Faerie, but he soon realized that was folly. The cook had volunteered to attend to Lady Aisla in her new home and had left for Ireland as well. Over the following months, Peter and John Drummond abandoned the manor house for locations unknown. House Drummond stood empty with the only known heir, Aisla Drummond, now Lady Aisla MacDuffee, living in Ireland with her devoted servant and cook.

Chapter 8

Mary O'Neil arrived in the raucous and dirty port city of New Orleans, Louisiana during the spring of 1877. It had taken her nearly a year to travel from her family's small cottage in Ireland to the nearest port and on to America. She had no idea how it was accomplished, only knowing that she would often awaken in a strange inn or tavern with a full belly, different clothes, and enough coins in her purse to allow her travels to continue. While in control of her faculties, she would walk the roads headed west to the sea, certain as a homing pigeon that she must make it across the ocean to freedom.

New Orleans was unlike anything that Mary had ever seen. She found herself feeling more out of her senses as nearly every other day she found herself in a different part of the city with coins and clothes that were not previously in her possession. She had given up questioning the whys and where-fors of her new life, resigned for the time being to simply flow along like a leaf caught in the whirlpool of a fast-moving stream.

Mary came to, as it were, one afternoon in a part of town that she had not yet visited. The lanes were narrow and often ankle-deep in mud, though a few did sport cleaner and more modern cobbled surfaces, and the buildings were multi-leveled with balconies and galleries dripping in ornate iron painted glossy black. She found herself sitting on the bottom step of the stoop of a large building with her battered suitcase cinched between her knees. Her purse, heavy against her thigh under her skirts, was filled with coins and in her hand was a scrap of a crudely printed leaflet advertising a position for a live-in. The street address on the paper matched the number on the building's column.

Accustomed as she had become with her loss of time and place, Mary found herself hoping that with a job, the lapses in awareness would soon stop.

She stood, smoothed her skirts, and bent to dust her boots off. Having tucked her unruly hair into her hat, she grasped the handle of the disreputable suitcase that had made the many journeys with her thus far and rapped on the tall wooden door of the house. A statuesque woman with a hawkish nose answered the knock and looked her up one side and down the other. After passing the housekeeper's test of who could be admitted, Mary was led into the cavernous foyer and her presence was announced to the lady of the house. It seemed that Mary was now employed, though she had no idea how this had happened. Once again, she simply accepted the situation and flowed along within the curious stream that had become her life.

Mary's time within the Delacour's household was, for the most part, acceptable. She was employed as a nanny and part-time housekeeper, jobs that she easily understood as both the eldest child within her own family cottage and during her time at the MacDuffee House back in Ireland. The small children in her care were enjoyable and well behaved, and the housekeeping was light. Her evenings were her own, and it was during those hours that she continued to experience gaps of missing time, though now with a terrifying twist. While her clothing no longer changed and her purse no longer held excess coins, other mysteries took their place. She would awaken in the early-morning hours blocks away from her Dumaine Street home, dirty and her lips stained red with blood. Whether the blood was her own, from another person, or from an animal she had no idea, but her fear grew as morning after morning the gruesome awakenings continued.

It was on a chilly autumn morning that she met Charlie Blanchard. It was before dawn, and the lack of light within the dirty back alley and the man's lack of sobriety allowed the wiry, dark-haired dock worker to miss the fact that Mary's mouth was smeared with blood and her well-made dress was splattered with mud. She would often think back to this fateful morning and wonder what her life would have become had she not met Charlie or if he had been sober enough to see the mess of blood on her face, but done was done as her Mam would say. Not only did she meet Charlie Blanchard, but she continued to do so for many more weeks to come hoping that the charming Irishman would be her salvation and way out of the nightmare that her life had become. While Charlie was funny and boisterous, Mary—inexperienced with men and the world in general—failed to put importance on the fact that while her new beau began the evenings as a gentleman and great fun, the nights more often than not ended with raised voices and the threats of a raised hand.

As the winter holidays came and went and the Mardi Gras season arrived with the beating of drums, the rattle of tambourines, and costumed figures parading under the wavering gas lamps of the French Quarter, Mary found herself several weeks pregnant. Though scared and unsure how to proceed, she accepted Charlie's request for marriage hoping still that he could still be her escape into a normal life. Mary moved in with her new husband to a small cottage on Saint Ann Street,   several blocks away from the Delacour's comfortable home . The cottage boasted only slightly more space than the drawing room of her former employer's house, but Mary made the best of it and set to create a home for her new family.

Her first child was born into the world in the sweltering early-summer heat that is June in New Orleans. While initially proud and happy to be a family man, Charlie soon grew tired of the constraints that fatherhood required, though not tired enough to abstain from the activities that actually resulted in fatherhood. Another baby was born into the small cottage in March, and baby after baby arrived one after the other, along with a set of twins, until October of 1882 saw the birth of Mary and Charlie's last child, Miriam Louis. It was a miracle that all six of Mary's children lived past birth, though not necessarily a blessing.

During the chaos of childbirth, child-rearing, too much drinking, too much fighting, and not enough food, Mary's loss of time continued. With multiple pregnancies, lack of nutrition, and youth, she sleepwalked through her life as the never-ending demands of nursing children, alcoholic tantrums, and the insatiable hunger of the Faerie drove her ever onward into the dark, dank alleys and courtyards of the French Quarter and further into semi-madness. Her nightmare that had begun in the rooms of Aisla Drummond MacDuffee continued unabated no matter the span of oceans or time.

As is so often the way of things, the eldest children of a chaotic home take on the role of parenting the youngest. Though this is rarely the best option, it is normally the only option. As her children grew and Charlie came home less often, Mary felt more lost within her mind, and she grew emotionally distanced from her brood. More times than not, the older children would chase the younger ones away from the wraith they called Mam. They regularly found her wrapped in shawls and huddled in the corner, reading endlessly from the small blue book she had brought over from her home in Ireland. She never read aloud and never shared what was contained within the book. When the sun went down and whatever food was at hand was set before the children, Mary would leave the house to roam the streets of the French Quarter only to return just before dawn dirty, disheveled, and smeared with blood. The children argued endlessly about what meat their mother sneaked out to feast upon, but none were brave enough to ask her directly.

In the sweltering heat of the French Quarter, the neighborhood scolds whispered and gossiped over bins of fruit and potatoes in the market and lines of laundry hanging limp in the heavy air. There was evil afoot and roaming about the lanes. Vagrants and gentlemen alike were found slumped in doorways and against lamp posts, their skin yellowed and with wounds like the scratches of a great cat along the length of their necks. These victims had no memory of what had befallen them. While most recovered, they remained weak and sickly. Physicians claimed this was but one of the many fevers bred in the dark waters of the mighty river that cradled the city, but most citizens knew better and shared whispers about blood-drinkers brought over from France that had been given refuge in the attics and gables throughout the French Quarter for over a century. Had one escaped?

The children of Mary Blanchard heard the rumors as they meandered along the back fences and market stalls, but they were too concerned with the daily tasks of eating and staying alive to pay the stories much mind. Then, everything changed abruptly.

Yellow fever, that perennial horror of the subtropical city, struck with a vengeance. The Blanchard household, having survived so much on Saint Ann Street, was about to be undone. Mary struggled valiantly to nurse the five of her children who fell ill, but it was of no use.

"Who is there?" called the slight woman in response to the abrupt rapping on the cottage's front door.

"Sisters from Charity Hospital, Mrs. Blanchard. We've come to take those with fever. Will you let us in?"

"One minute!" cried Mary, quickly straightening the coverlets and curtains, trying to make the shabby space look as nice as possible. In all her years there, guests had never called, and she was in a panic to not have the house look presentable.

Four of her children were delirious with fever, so far gone as to not know who they were or where they were. The eldest, Patrick, wasn't as far gone and watched as his mother tried desperately to make the cottage appear as something it was not.

"Here, Mam, let me help," he whispered as he steadied himself and stood up from the bed. Though the room spun, and his head pounded, the boy stood his ground, determined to be of help.

"And what would ye do, then?" came a sly and sneering voice not at all like his mother's. Patrick's arms pricked with gooseflesh as she turned to face him. Her eyes, normally a soft brown, were bright green and slanted. Her hair shone a burnished red when just minutes before it was a dull mahogany, silvered at the temples. But worse than all other features was the smile on the face of whatever was passing as his mother now. It was cruel, smart, and amused. Patrick took two steps back and sat heavily on the bed he had just crawled from.

"What are you?" he whispered, but the Baobhan Sidhe said nothing. Instead, it rummaged within his mother's shirtwaist chest and lifted out the battered old box that had been a part of her things for as long as he could remember.

"There's no key," he declared as forcibly as he could muster as the Sisters outside the front door continued to plead their entrance.

"Aye, but there is," laughed the green-eyed stranger as it felt along the top sill of the window and grasped the key concealed there years before. It winked with malicious amusement at Patrick and went to open the door to the Sisters waiting on the stoop.

"Come in, thank you," said Mary with a gentle smile to the nuns waiting outside.

"Mam?" squeaked Patrick.

"Yes, son?" and, indeed, it was his mother again.

Patrick had no idea where the green-eyed demon went, but there was no time to ask as the nuns bustled in, gathering the sickest of the children into a small cart and bidding Mary and Patrick to follow. Only Patrick noticed that Mary carried a small wooden box as they left the cottage bound for the new Charity Hospital.

"Mam, will we be back soon?" asked Patrick in a small voice full of fear and confusion.

"I don't know, son. I don't know," she replied softly, patting his thin face in a rare gesture of maternal love.

Most of the Blanchard family traveled to the new Charity Hospital on Common Street led by the Sisters who were tasked to find and retrieve fever victims. None of them would return. The only members of the family who would continue their desperate existence within the street, docks, and courtyards of the French Quarter were Charlie and his youngest daughter, Miriam, called Mimi.

Chapter 9

"Girl! There's a note left on the door. Read it to me," demanded Charlie Blanchard to his youngest daughter. It mattered not to him that she was just nine years old. Those old biddies, the nuns, had taken away his wife and the rest of his children. If the only one left to take care of him was a child of less than ten, then so be it.

Mimi walked carefully past her father, never sure when a hand would shoot out to cuff her on the ear or when a busted boot would insert itself between her feet, causing her to fall. Her father felt these actions were amusing and would laugh until he belched, leaving the small room wreaking of the cheap whiskey he always had at hand.

She retrieved the note tacked to their door, cursing again that she had been taught to read as it was just one more thing on the list of chores that Charlie demanded of her. While he was smart and cagey in his own way, Charlie Blanchard had never had a reason to learn to read and could only sign his name in the most rudimentary fashion. Mimi could both read and write but, at just nine years old, could not yet see the benefit of these skills.

"The effects and belongings of Mary Blanchard can be retrieved at the Common Street Charity Hospital. The deceased woman and her deceased children have been interred by the Sisters of Charity," Mimi read from the note. Her voice caught, and she read the small missive again, slower this time.

"They're all dead?" she asked her father in a small voice. "Why didn't you tell me?"

Charlie Blanchard, shrugged, stood, and walked out the door, leaving his only remaining child holding the letter that essentially left her orphaned.

Mimi, smart and streetwise child she was knew what 'deceased' meant but not the words 'effects' or 'interred', so she made no attempt to make the short walk to the hospital to see where her family was buried or to claim their meager belongings.

At the hospital, the young novice tasked with gathering the belongings of the dead patients opened the box labeled BLANCHARD. Inside were the grubby and broken shoes the family had worn when they arrived, a small bible that was given to one of the girls to read when it appeared she might recover from the fever, and an old wooden box and key that Mary O'Neil Blanchard brought along.

"I wonder why she brought this?" muttered the young woman.

Locating the key, she began to insert it into the old lock when her superior called for her to hurry and dispose of the excess boxes; the room was needed.

"I'm coming!" she called back and stuffed all but the wooden box back inside and closed the lid. She added the Blanchard effects to the sad pile of shoes, shawls, eyeglasses, and cheap jewelery from over one thousand departed yellow fever victims and left the gloomy storage room.

If asked, the young nun couldn't tell you why she kept the wooden box and its key aside from the pile or why she knew it to be so important that it not be burned with the rest, but she knew it as well as she knew her own name. Looking quickly around her, she ran quietly up the stairs to the vast storage spaces above the main floor and tucked the box under a pile of draperies by the gabled window farthest from the stairs.

"You'll be safe there," she whispered as she slipped back down the stairs with not a thought as to who would be safe and why she felt the need to make it so.

Chapter 10

Mimi woke at daybreak cold and hungry. The weather had turned overnight, frigid in its heavy dampness. At just under four feet tall, she was small and thin for an almost twelve-year-old girl, the result of both heredity and circumstance. Being forced to beg and steal for most of her food didn't allow for much in the way of hearty growth, and the cold and damp affected her more than it would someone with a bit more fat to them.

Shivering, Mimi wrapped one of her mother's shawls around her thin shoulders. She nudged the nest of rough woolen blankets under the bed that was shoved against the far wall, noting it had not been slept in. Feeling her face redden from frustration, the small girl thought of how much more comfortable the lumpy mattress would be than the wood floor and pile of hole-riddled blankets that made up her own bed. However, never knowing for certain when Charlie might make an appearance, the floor was safer in the long run. Her father, while not a danger to her in any way that would jeopardize her innocence, was quick with his fists and quicker yet when he was full of drink. And Charlie being drunk was about the only thing that Mimi could consistently count on. Best to sleep on the floor and be grateful that the bed remained unused.

Her bare feet stung from the cold, and her fingers smarted, making it difficult to light the lamp to illuminate the main room and give her enough light to set a fire in the fireplace. While other homes within the French Quarter were fed directly with gas that powered lights and small braziers inset within the mouths of the original wood-burning fireplaces, Charlie had not set aside enough of his earnings to outfit their home, leaving Mimi to struggle with hunger, light, and warmth. She had even heard that some of the larger homes and buildings had electricity for light, but it seemed a fairy tale to her. Mimi had become quite jaded in her less than a dozen years of life and chose to not engage in wishful thinking as it sapped the strength needed for survival. Why dream of what could be for other people when it would never happen for her?

She trimmed the lamp's wick and replaced the glass chimney to protect the fire from the drafts that blew in from the shuttered windows. Kneeling before the fireplace, she used a stick from the kindling pile to push through the grey ashes in search of a still-hot coal.

"Ah-ha! There you are!"

A smile as bright as the small flame of the kerosene lamp lit her face when a chunk of glowing ember was revealed in the farthest corner. Adding twists of scavenged paper fliers and handfuls of dead leaves from the sidewalks, she carefully coaxed flames from the orange-red orb. Soon enough, a cozy fire was dancing within the fireplace, and Mimi stood with her hands and feet as close as she dared, waiting for the stinging cold to loosen its grip on her fingers and toes.

She fed the fire the last of the kindling and set the old iron kettle, filled with water, on top. There was a wood-burning cookstove in the small kitchen, but it was a rare day when she had enough wood to fuel both the stove and the fireplace, and Mimi always prioritized the fireplace. Sitting cross-legged with her dress covering her bare feet for warmth, she waited for the water to heat and considered the day ahead. There was no more fuel for making a fire later in the day, so she would have to find wood, scraps of coal, or leaves. Mimi knew that unless she went out before the sun's rise, her chances of finding any errant coal chunks left on the pavements from that day's deliveries were slim to none. Dried leaves, sticks, and old wood were easier to find. Since the best place to gather wood was along the edges of the market, it would allow her a chance to find an apple or a potato that had happened to 'fall off' of a cart. She dearly wished there were ever an opportunity to find a praline candy that had 'fallen' from one of the old women's baskets, but the beatings they meted out to thieves were legendary, and Mimi had plenty of those to contend with at home.

"Fuel for the fire and some food for a soup. That should take care of the day, I suppose," Mimi said to herself.

As the old kettle began to hiss, she remembered that the last of the water had been used and added a trip to the neighbor's cistern to her list of tasks for the day. The housekeeper there kindly turned a blind eye to the dirty, skinny girl left to fend for herself in the cottage next door who sneaked over at nightfall to fill her bucket.

With her day mentally mapped out, Mimi stood and grasped the handle of the hot kettle with a scrap of cotton that had once been one of her brother's shirts. She carefully poured some of the hot water into the chipped and stained mug and added the last bits of a withered apple. As the old fruit softened, it released a homey smell that made Mimi's stomach constrict painfully. She slowly sipped the barely-flavored water, feeling it pool in the bottom of her empty belly and quell the hunger pangs for the time being. When she had emptied the mug of water, she scooped the sodden bits of apple from the bottom of the cup with her fingers and sucked every last bit into her mouth, relishing the sweetness of the fruit and leathery chewiness of the skin.

Deciding to sacrifice the last bit of water in the kettle, Mimi plugged the sink and emptied the last of the kettle's contents into the stained porcelain basin. Using the same scrap of cotton that had just been employed as a hot pad, the small child dipped it into the warm water and scrubbed the last few days of grime from her face, hands, and her bare feet. Scurrying over into the central room where the fire burned high, she warmed her wet skin and felt it prickle as the water evaporated in the heat that radiated from the fireplace. Mimi smiled and felt, if not happy, at least content. She was warm, somewhat clean, and the complaints from her stomach had stopped for now.

Opening the louvered shutters revealed the sun had fully risen over the balconies and roofs of her neighborhood, and the sounds of the street cars clacking away along with the ringing of horse's hooves on the street's cobblestones attested to a day underway.

She carefully banked the fire, trimmed the oil lamp, and grabbed her mother's old market basket, leaving the house to find the necessary supplies for her continued survival. Mimi sighed in resignation at the sight of her newly washed feet, wishing that a pair of shoes and some woolen stockings that fit her would find their way into her basket. It would be nice to have warm and clean toes for more than a few minutes at a time.

Mimi walked slowly through the cold morning air toward the river and the large market. Here and there, she stopped to pick up a handful of dried leaves, some twigs, and the occasional pebble of coal that had rolled into the gutter. The voices of the Italian families that had become ubiquitous within the fifteen-block area were both melodic and dramatic. Mimi loved how they floated over her head from gallery to gallery—sounds as colorful as exotic birds—but knew that Charlie and his Irish buddies despised the newest immigrants, feeling they were competition for jobs and space within the cramped neighborhoods.

The large pillars of the market beckoned her onward, and the voices of the French, Italian, Irish, and American citizens all blended into one lullaby with the counterpoint of the singsong of the West Indies and its surrounding islands. Mimi walked slowly, making herself as insignificant as possible, with the ultimate goal of going completely unseen by the other shoppers and market vendors.

Watching carefully as a fat butcher argued with a black servant sent into the market to shop for a wealthy house, Mimi carefully scooped a bit of bacon fat into her basket and covered it with some of the dried leaves, watching the butcher the entire time to ensure that his eyes remained firmly on the angry woman accusing him of selling rancid chicken as fresh. Mimi licked a bit of the bacon grease from her fingers and sighed blissfully as the pungent oil coated her tongue. She turned a corner and walked along the line of stalls nearest to the levy. The Italian ladies were beautiful with their large, dark eyes and glossy hair, and their vegetable stalls looked like the paintings that Mimi had seen in the nicer homes as she walked by the lit windows at night. She marveled at the radishes, arranged like bouquets of small roses, and the carrots bunched together to showcase the vibrant orange of their flesh. Mimi carefully edged a potato and onion into her basket as an older, raven-haired woman chatted with another customer at the end of the stall. Leaving the beautiful vegetables to their equally beautiful vendors, she turned to walk behind them where scraps of vegetable tops, potato peelings, and wooden slats from crates were tossed along the river's man-made embankment. Mimi joined the usual gang of children, most also shoe-less and with the most rudimentary clothing, as they scavenged for whatever discarded fuel and food could be found in the rubble and dirt. There was no laughter or conversation from the children, so focused were they on gathering what small things would provide food and warmth for another day or two.

She switched her basket to her other arm as the ache turned to pain. She was happy she had found enough food and supplies for the basket to be heavy, but the walk home was going to be slow-going. It had taken the better part of the day, but she had managed to find enough vegetable leavings for a soup that, flavored with the bacon grease, would fill her belly not only tonight but tomorrow morning, too. There weren't as many broken pieces and bits of wooden crates as she would have liked, but there were enough scraps of kindling in the basket for a couple of small fires to warm her and cook her soup. She thought back on the gaggle of children that searched the levy as she did. She knew she had more than most because she had fewer people to feed and keep warm. Being alone meant she didn't have to share her supplies. The realization cut; she would have gladly gathered everything needed to feed her siblings and mother.

As the tears rolled down her face and turned her world blurry, she stopped to wipe her eyes. The sun was dipping below the pitched roofs of the French Quarter, and mothers called for their children to come home. Mimi's heart hurt, and the tears flowed once again. Hitching in a breath to calm her sudden release of emotion, the small girl felt a chill that had nothing to do with the cool evening air. Her street-urchin life had, by necessity, provided her with the instincts of prey animals, like rabbits or mice, and these instincts were now telling her that something was wrong. Very wrong. She set her basket down and sat on the curb as nonchalantly as possible for a scared and lonely girl. She looked around but could find nothing amiss. The gas lamps were flickering in the gathering purple twilight, children were running home for their supper, and the street cars were rattling along their tracks the same as always. But the hairs prickling on her arms and neck told her that, no matter the normalcy of her surroundings, there was danger.

Clip-clop. Clip-clop.

Mimi heard the slow advance of hooves on pavement, but who would be riding a horse on the sidewalk?

Clip-clop. Clip-clop.

The hairs on Mimi's scalp rose painfully as she realized that the sound she heard was hooves—but only two, not four. Horses and mules have four feet. Nothing that she knew of had two and made that sound.

Like many other creatures that know they are prey, Mimi froze. She didn't want to. In fact, every part of her was screaming to run. Run now! But her muscles wouldn't comply. She sat on the curb, shaking and wide-eyed, as whatever walked on two cloven feet moved closer and closer.

Clip-clop. Clip-clop.

Then, it stopped. And still, she couldn't move.

"Mmmmmm, I smell an old friend," purred a female voice close to her ear. The accent was vaguely Irish like her father's and mother's but with a slightly different cadence. The sly amusement in the unhurried words made Mimi's skin crawl.

"I don't suppose ye would know my friend Mary, would ye now?" purred the unknown woman from just behind Mimi's trembling body.

The terrified girl screwed her eyes shut and clamped her mouth closed to stop the scream that threatened to escape her lips. She was certain that to see or speak to this thing would spell her doom. Unable to run, she chose to hide the creature from her sight instead.

"Don't worry, my dearie. We don't need to talk just yet. I have time, lots of time," and with a throaty chuckle, the thing that walked on hooves moved past her and into the shadows between the closely built houses.

Clip-clop. Clip-clop. Clip-clop.

Mimi didn't open her eyes or move a muscle until she could no longer hear the creature's hooves. It seemed an eternity.

When she finally felt safe enough to open her eyes, it was dark. The gas lamps made shadows dance along the street. Mimi felt neither the heaviness of the basket nor the cold on her bare feet as she ran headlong down the sidewalk to the relative safety of her home.

Chapter 11

Bennette stood just to the left of the mirror that hung on an obscure wall within the hospital's offices. He watched as the young hospital worker grabbed the Blanchard Box and ran up the attic stairs with it tucked securely under her grey-clad arm, the key clutched tightly in her hand.

His heart sank. When he realized that Mary Blanchard—and the majority of her family—had taken ill with fever and were being relocated to the nearby hospital, he thought for certain that the Baobhan Sidhe would die with its host. The box with its homeland's earth had been unseen for so long. Bennette had relied on seeing through mirrors, and that was a deadly mistake. Just like in Ireland and Scotland, the poor in America often didn't have mirrors. His ability to keep tabs on the Fae that he had vowed to destroy had been severely compromised.

Another fatal mistake was assuming that the creature couldn't walk on its own without a human host. His elder Brothers dispelled that erroneous thought and emphasized what a calamity it was to have the Fae free and loose within the dark warrens and alleyways of America's French Quarter.

"But when I witnessed the cook's ritual, the creature said it needed a host to be free!" cried the distraught Bennette as two of the elder monks watched him with sympathy.

"No, my son," replied the oldest of the monks. "What the creature said was that it needed blood to be free. Having a host simply gave it a convenient way to feed. The host is not necessary for the Baobhan Sidhe to thrive.

Once the cook provided the box with the soil of the Fae's homeland, it had a place to rest and gather its strength should a host not be available or desired."

"I have failed miserably," moaned Bennett. "Why can't I just end this now by using the In-Between to go back before the creature was called forth? I can save my Aisla and undoubtedly countless more souls from the nightmare that is this creature."

"My dear Brother," began the elder named John, "it's not that it can't be done but that it would leave you in a never-ending spiral of trying to adjust and re-adjust different scenarios. Remember your training. 'Magic, Prayer, and Energy all follow the path of least resistance.' This is not just a maxim for sending the will out but a reminder of a path already begun. It is fraught with danger to attempt to undo that which has begun. The way to success is to observe and influence the flow of situations and energy into a result that is harmonious. There are no shortcuts."

"Is the In-Between not a shortcut?" countered Bennette.

Brother John smiled, "The In-Between is a realm and space complete unto itself, just as a road is its own space. While it may be used to reach another point, one must still accept that it is a road. Does that make sense, my son?"

"No," replied Bennette snappishly. "What is the point of the In-Between if it is not a shortcut?"

"What is the point of a road?" countered Brother John. "We have provided you with instruction, learning, and philosophy regarding the Mysteries. Few are ever afforded this honor, Brother Bennette. Fewer yet have the internal strength to add personal insight and practical application to these Mysteries. Will you?"

And with that, the elders left the candle-lit chamber hidden deep within the recesses of the monastery, leaving Bennette to alternately seethe and ponder his predicament.

"What is a road, indeed," muttered Bennette as he carefully stepped away from the small glass pane that showed only an empty hospital corridor in New Orleans. The monk moved back to the flickering candlelight that danced through the violet mists to the safety and refuge of the monastery. His Aisla was gone—dead in Ireland. The cook was, presumably, the de facto Lady of House Drummond having fulfilled the Fae's demands. He knew he could peer through the mirror within the Drummond House's sitting room for confirmation, but it meant little to him now. Fighting despair and melancholy, he stepped into the stone chamber that had served as his college of the Mysteries, a place of comfort and fear, a room of acceptance and incredulity. Here he would rest and meditate on how best to influence the coming events that would spell the end of the Baobhan Sidhe.

Chapter 12

Mimi stretched her legs and felt the damp, early-May air against her bare feet. The pre-dawn morning was pleasant ahead of the heaviness and heat that would descend upon the streets in just a few short hours. Mimi's eyes were sore and crusted from the tears shed after the long, sleepless night—compliments of Charlie. Despite the previous evening, she felt a twinge of contentment at the lack of smothering humidity.

Mimi had grown accustomed to her father roaming in and out of the small cottage. As such, she had long ago moved her nest of blankets out of the bedroom and next to the fireplace. This arrangement offered additional warmth during the chilly winter evenings and a small amount of privacy as her drunk and stumbling father unerringly made right for the bed before collapsing in a fetid whiskey haze. Mimi had been stepped on and tripped over one too many times. She found her fireside sleeping arrangements the most comfortable so far.

Feeling stiff and sore, eyes swollen from crying and lack of sleep, the thin sixteen-year-old held the weariness and wariness of her life like a shield. There was nothing soft about Mimi Blanchard, not in the lankiness of her limbs, the sharpness of her cheekbones, or the jaded gaze of her large eyes. Softness was a luxury born of health, wealth, and safety—she was privy to none of these benefits.

As she poured water into the kettle for her tea, she glanced across into the adjoining room where Charlie lay sprawled across the thin mattress, mouth open and snoring loudly. More and more often, he came back to the Saint Ann Street cottage, drunk, raving, and panicked. He carried on about creatures hiding in the shadows with yellow skin and sharp teeth and a woman who followed him with red hair and long fingernails. He swore that it wasn't the whiskey that caused him to hear phantom horses tracking his own footfalls as he wandered from bar-to-bar alternating between evasion and liquid escape. Last night's episode had been the worst of them so far. In the deep night between sunset and dawn, she was jolted awake to the terror-filled screams of her father just outside the cottage.

"NO! Get back! Ye've a plague, I know it! No, stay away from me!"

His cries grew louder as he made his way to the front door, bursting through with a wail born of the fear that drove him home and the relief of making it to safety.

"Charlie! Stop! Stop now or the police will come!" cried Mimi, fighting for a stern voice. She knew the panic radiating from her drunk and raving father was making its way into her voice as well.

"Girl, don't ye be tellin' me! There are monsters and sickness about. If that's not a reason to yell then I don't know what is!" slurred her father who stood unsteadily before her, gathering his breath and releasing it in great gusts of alcohol-infused waves.

"You're drunk, as always. Those with the fever don't have the strength to chase you down, Charlie. Why would they want to, anyway? What can you do for them?" spat Mimi at the disheveled figure in front of her.

His dark hair, salted through now with grey, stood up in dirty spikes. His eyes, once a sparkling blue, had sunk and were blurry with the abuse he subjected his body to day after day, night after night. His shirt, once a respectable cream color, was splattered with heaven knows what and stained dark under the arms and along the collar.

"You can't even take care of yourself," she hissed as she moved past him to coax a bit of flame from the previously banked fire.

"You think you're so smart, don't you, girl?" slurred Charlie, watching her as she stood before the fireplace. "If you're so smart, so much better than me, then tell me what these are!"

Mimi smelled the mixture of old whiskey, cheap cologne, and unwashed clothes as her father moved closer to her. The sharp jab he landed between her shoulder blades forced her to turn around and face him, the person she had been saddled with since the loss of her mother and siblings.

Charlie yanked aside the dirt-encrusted collar of his shirt to expose his neck. Running straight down from his hairline—through the rings of dirt that had settled within the folds of his skin and jumping over his jutting collarbones—were deep scratches and gouges. Some fresh and oozing blood and some healed, layered one over the other.

"Don't scratch the lice, Charlie. Bathe on occasion, and that won't happen," sighed Mimi, sounding more adult and responsible than her father who wobbled and swayed in front of her.

"'Tis not lice!" spat the bleary-eyed man, completely unaware of the irony in his show of pride. "'Tis the monster! She waits till I've had a seat to rest my feet, and then she does this and licks the blood from me neck, too!"

"Do you have any idea how that sounds? Why not just get up out of the gutter and walk away?"

"I can't," stammered the beleaguered man, understanding even through the haze of drink that his daughter thought he was mad.

"She does…something. My mind gets all fuzzy. I kind of drift away, not really caring at all what she does 'till she's gone. Then my neck burns like a hot iron were put to it."

"That's called *drunk*, Charlie. No women are interested in accosting you. It's all from the inside of the bottle," replied Mimi with a weary sigh. She almost preferred the cantankerous and belligerent Charlie to the scared and confused version.

"Well, then what of the creatures that avoid the streetlamps? The skinny things with yellowed skin and long, sharp teeth?"

"Probably fever victims that have been put out by their families. It would truly be difficult to tell which was sicker—you, with your booze-fuelled visions, or them and their fever-wracked bodies wasting away and waiting to die."

Seeming to not hear her any longer, Charlie gazed over Mimi's shoulder at visions of a life lived in another time and in another country where he was taught the rules and rituals to avoid the things that walked the night and strayed from the light.

Mimi looked him over as his blue eyes, now clear and coherent, swung back and rested on her face.

"Something is here, Miriam. Something that knows us and will destroy us. Your mother wasn't strong enough, and God knows I'm not. Have a care, girl. Learn the

Old Ways, and maybe you'll be strong enough to survive it."

And her father's blue eyes clouded over again. He stepped around her, running his grimy fingers over the deep gashes on his neck. As he collapsed onto the bed, Mimi's legs gave way. She dropped cross-legged onto the hearth, tears running freely down her face. The tiniest glimpse of who her father once was, of who he could be, broke her heart. She cried for hours, tears of anger, tears of frustration, and tears of loss. Finally, her eyes swollen and her tears dried up, Mimi curled up on her blankets in front of the guttering fire with thoughts of monsters, both human and not, flitting through her exhausted mind.

The present intruded on her memories of the previous night by way of the shrill whistle of the kettle. Sighing, she added a twist of cheesecloth filled with an assortment of aromatics and herbs scavenged from the neighbors' gardens. Most turned a blind eye to her occasional thievery, and for that, she was grateful. As her tea steeped, she glanced again at the ruined man on the bed.

"He'll be out for hours yet," she muttered to herself as she wiped out the only mug in the house, stained and chipped as it was.

Mimi sat on her small stoop and watched as the neighborhood around her came to life. She sipped her mug of tea and considered the previous night. Charlie's drunken rambling made her tired, but she was used to it. The brief moment of clarity, however, and his warnings about 'things that walked the night' had completely thrown her and forced her to unearth a half-remembered encounter from years back of the thing that walked on two hooves. The creature with a woman's voice had scared her enough that she ran as fast as she could back to the safety of her house, much as Charlie had been doing these past few months. Were his fears truly the result of a brain thoroughly soaked in whiskey, or was the mind—unmoored by alcohol—able to see more of what lurked in the night-time streets of the French Quarter? Mimi felt her aloneness keenly as she realized that there was no one in her life that she could ask. Aside from Charlie, she was on her own.

As she drained the last of the weak herbal tea from her mug, Mimi realized the vision of who her father could be in another life had broken something within her. The understanding that she was completely alone settled around her like a mantle. Rather than feeling smothering or sad, the longer she sat and truly felt her aloneness, she began to feel stronger. Waiting for her father to be a father, or even an adult, would no longer serve her. For all intents and purposes, the small cottage was hers. Charlie was simply an occasional visitor. At just sixteen years old, Miriam

Blanchard decided she was an adult. The desperate hand-to-mouth existence that Charlie had dropped her into from early childhood was done. It was time to find a job.

Chapter 13

Mimi smoothed her apron over her skirt and hefted the tray full of drinks high over her head as she navigated the crowded dining room, headed to the table of smartly dressed men by the front window. She had decided on this restaurant to inquire about a cook's job due to its proximity to the large 'houses' in the neighborhood nicknamed Storyville. Ironically, the owners wouldn't hire her as a cook as it would be 'unseemly.' Instead, she was offered a job as a waitress. While initially disappointed, Mimi found this allowed her generous tips from the male patrons and afforded her an excellent opportunity to hone her considerable skills as a petty thief.

"Well, hello there! Aren't you a pretty little thing?!" bellowed the obvious leader of the group of male patrons. His fellows all chuckled, riding the general atmosphere of the promise of good times and favors that were plentiful in the brothels and smaller 'cribs' located within the blocks between Canal and Basin Streets. Mimi was street smart and intuitive, and she knew she could cash in on the *idea* of what Storyville offered without having to actually engage in the activities. She also realized early on that, should she choose to go that route, the way was wide open for her. However, after having her epiphany after Charlie's few moments of lucidity, the idea of being hemmed in and controlled by another person for longer than an eight-hour work shift didn't appeal to her. Her independence, so far, had been hard-won, and she was loath to give it up to a Madam who would take most of her earnings.

She choked back a squeak and managed to not dump the tray of drinks in the lap of a particularly portly gentleman when he squeezed her backside as she set the glasses on the table. As much as it annoyed her, she rearranged her features to show nothing but amusement and a vague look of promise. Her coy attitude was rewarded with a smarmy wink by the offender. A tinkling laugh and a sparkle of her eyes kept his attention on her face as her hand snaked into his pocket and deftly removed a clip of folded cash. Patting him on the arm after slipping her ill-gotten gains into her apron pocket sealed the deal, though not at all in the way that the gentleman imagined. In fact, by the time Mimi was safely at home later that evening, her customer would be picking himself up out of the dirty gutter in front of one of the largest and most opulent brothels where he would be tossed when it became apparent he had no cash with which to pay for the lady he had attempted to hire.

"You, dear girl, need some fattening up!" roared the man as he patted her behind. "Get you some meat on those bones!"

The table laughed and nudged each other in the ribs. Mimi maintained her simpering look of forced femininity while setting down the rest of the table's drinks. Her laugh as she walked away from the group was genuine as she fingered the fat roll of bills she took as payment for the groping.

While not exactly scrupulous, Mimi did have a code, of sorts, that she strove to live by. She didn't steal from anyone who looked as poor as herself unless absolutely necessary, and she wouldn't cause physical harm unless it was in self-defense. Miriam Blanchard was cagey enough to keep options open that ensured her survival; Charlie had taught her well. The last gift from her father was her complete abstinence from alcohol. She had seen more than enough at home and on the streets of the French Quarter of what whiskey could do to a man or woman. She wanted no part of it and so kept her vices to tobacco and coffee or tea.

As she was stashing the wad of cash in her coat pocket, the cook bellowed for her to come and grab her plates of food that had been languishing in the kitchen as she amused herself by making false promises to the businessmen at the front window table. Wanting to cash in on the leader's tip that would add to her bottom dollar of the evening, Mimi stuffed her coat back into the rack among her coworkers' and hurried to the window separating the small dining room from the even smaller kitchen.

"Jayzus, Mimi! Get this crap outta my window! It's getting cold—same as the rest of the plates waiting their turn! Step it up!"

Mimi bobbed her head in acknowledgment, keeping her eyes downcast. Quickly arranging the plates on her tray, she shot a quick look back at the cook who glared at her as he stacked the next order in the window and called for its attending waitress. Mimi didn't like the cook, and the cook didn't like Mimi. Both were fine in that arrangement. They both knew that one word from the cook and Mimi would be sent packing, so she stayed quiet and meek and avoided any confrontation that could result in her unemployment.

Avoiding the customer who had groped her, Mimi hoped the table would allow her to put their plates down and leave. As the last plate was placed in front of a younger man with an impressive mustache, Mimi sighed with relief—she finished her shift unmolested.

As she folded her apron and put on her coat, Mimi wrapped her fingers around her earnings, both legitimate and not, that sat fat and promising within her pocket. It was all she could do to not stop at the nearest empty table and sit down to count it. She was positive she had made an impressive amount today.

As the lights in the dining room dimmed and the clanking and crashing, along with no small amount of cursing, flowed from the kitchen, Mimi stepped outside into the chilly evening. The sky above the peaked roofs and gables of the French Quarter shone violet as the sun set, making it seem as if night rose from the streets and lanes rather than fell from the sky in the absence of the sun.

She stopped in an alcove, s recessed entrance to the building next to the restaurant and removed the fat wad of cash from her pocket. Freeing the roll of bills from the businessman's money clip, she smoothed her money into a flat packet and slipped it into her shoe. Mimi held the money clip up to a streetlamp. It was made from cheap metal, not real silver, so she tossed it into the gutter and began her walk home.

She passed familiar buildings and houses, and mists rose from the river that flowed silently past just a few blocks away. The city's sounds and people's voices were at once muffled and jarringly distinct. The call of mothers to their roaming children mixed with the jingle of carriages, the clanking of street cars, and the occasional automobile quieted as she moved further into the interior of the French Quarter. The gas lamps that dotted the street corners and doorways flickered in the gathering darkness.

Mimi kept her eyes resolutely forward and repeated her admonishments to Charlie back to herself. They sounded just as hollow now as they did two years ago as wraith-like creatures slunk along the edges of the light.

Turning the corner from Royal Street, she came upon a hunched figure with a head that was mostly bald if not for the tufts of scraggly hair stuck here and there to its skull. Its eyes were sunken but shining bright with sickness. The thing hissed in surprise, its open mouth showing alarmingly long teeth due to its inflamed and receded gums. The creature held one arm out to her, imploring, and Mimi bolted in fear across the street into a pool of lamplight. The yellow-skinned thing hunched its back and hissed in frustration, unable or unwilling to follow.

Mimi stood silent and shaking in the haven of gaslight for a long while after the thing — maybe a fever victim, maybe not — continued its slinking walk within the shadows down Saint Ann and disappeared into the narrow warren of side streets.

When she finally moved out of the lamp's safety and made it to her cottage, she bolted the louvered shutters at the front door and drew the makeshift curtains over the windows. She lit a kerosine lamp and sipped at a mug of water until her heart stopped hammering against her ribs and the tears stopped flowing down her cheeks. She hadn't seen Charlie in over a year and suddenly found herself missing him desperately.

Dawn found her with her head cradled in her arms, asleep at the small table. The lamp had burned down hours before.

Chapter 14

As Mimi lived her adult life, thriving by a poor orphan's standards, Bennette continued his mission as a guardian, of sorts, and would-be assassin. Both of these roles were completely self-imposed, and his Brothers at the monastery had long ago accepted that Bennette was a member of their order in name only. After the loss of Aisla and Mary to the Baobhan Sidhe, Bennette vowed he would put an end to the Fae. Furthermore, he knew that Mary's child, Mimi, would be instrumental in helping him.

Bennette was often forced to leave the sanctuary of his oak tree in the In-Between and walk among the citizens of the French Quarter. Bennette's vision was long thanks to his unique perspective, and he needed to move Mimi along the path that best suited his plans to achieve his goal. It meant little to him that he was using her as a pawn in his personal chess game. For Brother Bennette, the means justify the ends when the greater good is at stake.

Bennette strolled along the quiet paths of the square that fronted St. Louis Cathedral. The morning mists from the nearby river rose and dissipated with the gathering strength of the sun. He found the cathedral was the perfect gateway for his movements between Mimi's time and the In-Between; there were several mirrors within the large building, and his robes gathered no undue attention.

His steps echoed off the church's exterior walls on either side of the narrow alley that led to Rue Royal. Bennette stopped to adjust the small, framed mirror he carried under one arm. While the cathedral offered him safe entry and exit, he was still not able to see Mimi within her home. He planned to rectify that.

The service alley was devoid of pedestrians this early in the morning, and Bennette made the bustle of Royal Street in record time where carriages and autos rumbled and clanked past on their way to offices and stores that would soon open for the day's business. The tall, robed monk walked a few blocks up the street, skirting horse dung and standing water left from the night before, and turned onto Saint Ann Street. It was quieter in the residential area where households might be awake but had yet to emerge and begin their public day. He slowed his pace accordingly. The heaviness of the air and the quiet of the cheek-by-jowl homes quelled the need to walk quickly suggesting, instead, a leisurely stroll of which he was more than happy to oblige.

The grey and peeling exterior of Mimi's cottage stood out from its neighbors with their clean paint and crisp trim. Bennette stopped several doors before his intended destination and glanced surreptitiously about to ensure no one was watching him. No shutters moved, and no figures stood in doorways. Bennette strolled as casually as possible up to Mimi's shuttered front door where he propped the small mirror at the base of her stoop then smoothly continued along his way. Knowing her love of found and ill-gotten treasures, Bennette didn't doubt that Mimi would snatch up the mirror and add it to her cache of meager possessions.

After completing his first task of the day, Bennette walked further up the block toward the bounding street that signaled the end of the French Quarter then looped back around to the cathedral. The hustle and bustle of Mimi's time invigorated and enchanted him, and he chose to indulge himself with a longer stay before he escaped back into the twilight mists of the In-Between. No matter the warnings and admonishments of his Brothers and elders, Bennette was fully committed to exerting his will on the events of this time in order to weave together the necessary happenings that allowed for the retribution he sought. The evils done by the Faerie called the Baobhan Sidhe must be stopped from ever happening again and paid for in full.

As Bennette walked the streets that had come to life with the full brightness of the day, Mimi opened the louvered shutters that served as her front door. The morning's relative coolness flowed in and brushed away the stale overnight air that had gathered within her house. Blinded by the strike of the sun's ray on the mirror's glass, she shielded her eyes with the back of her hand and squatted down to inspect what caused the glare.

"Oh, my!" exclaimed the young woman in delight as she held the oval mirror up. Her face, fresh from a fairly decent night's sleep and a recent splash of cool water, looked pink-cheeked and youthful within the glass. At just twenty years old, Mimi was attractive but not as curvy as her forebears due to her past circumstances. Though, with her job at the restaurant and her recent dedication to making an actual life for herself beyond the hand-to-mouth existence that had been her childhood, her face was not as pinched and her arms not as thin as they once were. Her eyes, dark and wide, remained watchful and wary and would likely not change.

Looking to make sure the unlikely gift wasn't a trap, the street-wise Mimi slipped quickly back inside her home and latched the shutters just in case the owner of the mirror were to appear and accuse her of theft. While she knew she hadn't stolen the looking glass, she had stolen enough other objects and items over the years to validate her concerns.

Mimi decided her new mirror should go into the common front room where her small table and chairs were. Little by little, the small space took on the appearance of the room she imagined her mother would have wanted. As she slipped the framed glass over a tack in the plaster wall, it reflected back her face and the green herbs behind her that she had cut from the neighbor's garden and re-planted in the cast-off coffee cans that were gleaned from the gutters. She smiled as she imagined the addition of pretty curtains and a rug. How she would add them, she had no idea. But she was determined to make a life for herself that Charlie couldn't sully.

Settling back against his beloved oak tree's massive trunk, Bennette took a deep breath and steadied himself. No matter how often he made the trip into and out of the In-Between, it still took a bit of time for his body to adjust. As his heartbeat slowed and the clamminess on his palms dried up, the young man breathed deeply and stood to his full height. Centering his energy, he reached out with his thoughts until he felt the particular vibration that was Mimi. Once established, he brought to mind a clear image of the mirror he had left on her stoop just a few short hours ago, or hundreds of years in the future, or thousands of years in the past—time being especially relative where he stood.

The image solidified within his mind and the In-Between; Bennette successfully established a clear and accessible portal to Mimi. He watched as the young woman smiled into the glass. He saw the curtains and rugs that she imagined would decorate her home. As she stepped away, he was left with an image of her window and the scraggly potted herbs on its sill.

Chapter 15

"Oh! I'm so sorry. Please excuse me!" exclaimed the young woman, blushing furiously as she fell into the well-dressed gentleman waiting to cross Basin Street.

"Hold on there, darling," chortled Mimi's mark. "You don't want to mess your pretty dress in all of this mud!"

It had rained incessantly for the last three days, and her would-be rescuer pointed to the ankle-deep puddles of murky water that covered the gutters and walkways of the street and its sidewalks.

"Thank you so much!" breathed Mimi in an amazing display of helplessness. "I'm so glad that you were here! I must've slipped on something," she continued as she coyly held up a slim leg, baring one stockinged ankle and calf in an interesting display of inspecting her shoe.

As expected, the man on which she leaned took the opportunity to ogle her leg that would normally be covered in layers of skirts, giving Mimi the chance to move her hand ever so slightly from his arm and around to his jacket pocket where she deftly removed his money clip. Again, she pretended to nearly slip and disguised the theft as the valiant if not somewhat dim-witted, man helped her stand upright again, and the deed was done. Mimi had made more cash in just two minutes of showmanship than a week at the restaurant would bring in.

"Say, now! How about you and I go for a cup of coffee and get to know each other a little bit, eh?" he suggested as Mimi smoothed her skirts and righted the small straw boater that sat pinned at a jaunty angle on her chestnut up-do.

Mimi wasn't surprised by the suggestion. A lone young woman in this particular part of the city could easily be seen as a working girl for one of the large brothels or an independent prostitute looking to add to her purse with favors. Mimi, however, was a thief—not a whore—and so crisply declined the offer of coffee, and its insinuation of more, and quickly escaped onto one of the smaller side streets.

"That was quite the display back there."

Mimi jumped and almost fell for real as an arm slipped through hers and the owner matched her steps, seamlessly falling into line with her as she turned onto Rue Royal.

Mimi stopped and turned to face the woman who had witnessed the pickpocket and recognized it for what it was.

"Who are you, and why are you touching me?" Mimi asked in a low voice.

"Settle yourself, darling," crooned the young woman, matching Mimi's tone exactly. She stopped walking, forcing Mimi to do the same as their arms were still linked, and looked directly at her.

Mimi met the woman's gaze. Her unwanted walking companion had the beautiful café au lait complexion of les gens de couleur libre, or the Free People of Color, and her glossy black hair was fashioned into thick curls sectioned into five fat rolls that hung around her head and framed her face. The woman wore no hat, but the lack of decor was made up for by the bright red and white-striped shirtwaist and skirt that should have looked like a circus tent but instead hugged the curves of the young woman's body in a way that wouldn't have been possible on most women.

Removing her arm from the other woman's crooked elbow, Mimi snapped her parasol up in a display of annoyance.

"Who are you?" Mimi pressed again.

"I'm Vera. It's nice to meet you."

"We haven't met. You've accosted me," replied Mimi in a clipped tone that should have sent Vera on her way, but the opposite seemed to have happened.

"Well, tell me your name, and then we shall have met!" replied Vera with a throaty laugh and a flash of white teeth in her generous mouth.

Mimi eyed her companion with suspicion. She was really quite lovely and very well dressed. Her speech was educated and her mannerism cultured, yet she spied Mimi's theft of the man's money clip from a block away. None of it added up, and Mimi was loath to give too much information away to this stranger who had the eye of a thief but the dress of a fine lady.

"I'm Miriam, called Mimi," she replied stiffly, not offering her hand nor any extra information.

"Hello, Miriam-called-Mimi," smiled Vera, her voice dripping with amusement. "We are now formally acquainted. Shall we walk and you can tell me all about the fast work you did on that poor man's money?"

"I haven't the faintest idea of what you are talking about," defended Mimi as Vera once again took her arm and steered them both down the sidewalk, the shadow of Mimi's parasol shielding them both from the sun's subtropical rays.

"You can stop the act now," said Vera, her voice just a note harder, but Mimi caught it just the same. "I saw you lift the man's money and stash it in your sleeve. It was done smooth as you please. Who trained you?"

Mimi glanced sideways at the woman who walked next to her, unsure if they were now friends or if she was about to have her newly acquired cash taken from her.

"What do you want?"

"I want you to answer me. Who trained you, and who are you working with?" Vera asked.

"No one trained me," replied Mimi, purposely answering only half of the question.

Vera stopped walking and turned to face Mimi.

"How did you know to approach that particular gentleman?"

Mimi quickly hid her surprise at the question. It was not at all what she expected and honestly wasn't sure how to answer it.

"What color did you see?" Vera shot the question out whip-fast, and Mimi replied before she had a chance to think about the answer or the wisdom in providing it.

"Dull blue."

"I knew it!" Vera's mouth stretched into a wide grin full of triumph and delight. "You can see! When I saw your Light, I thought you might be able to. But when you targeted that dullard, I was certain! Not that your technique isn't top-notch, it really is! But knowing that that poor man couldn't think his way out of a brown paper sack certainly made the job easier, didn't it?"

Mimi stood staring at Vera, her mouth hanging open in surprise.

"What on earth are you talking about!?" she hissed, looking around at the pedestrians walking past them on the busy street.

Had anyone heard this nonsense about 'seeing?' What about her pickpocket technique? The last thing she needed was to answer questions about the money in her sleeve. She could claim to be a prostitute, but Royal Street was beyond the boundaries of Storyville, and that itself would cause her trouble.

"You know full well what I'm talking about," Vera replied as she took Mimi's arm once again and started up Royal toward Canal Street.

"I asked you what color you saw, and you said 'dull blue.' That is exactly what I saw shining around the man on the corner, though I probably would have described it as 'dirty blue' or 'grey blue.' Either way, his color showed him to be not entirely bright, and his clothing said that, while not smart, he had more than enough cash to spare. Very good choice, indeed," Vera bobbed her head firmly signaling her approval of Mimi's choice in victims.

Mimi didn't answer, her head swimming from the sudden influx of thoughts and the overwhelming chatter of her walking companion. Vera never stopped talking. If she thought it, she said it. Mimi had never experienced anything like it before. Even her coworkers at the restaurant didn't go on to this extent. Conversation occurred when tables were slow, but not like this. Mimi's head throbbed.

"Please, stop."

Vera stopped talking mid-sentence and looked over at Mimi for the first time since resuming their stroll several blocks back.

"What's wrong," she asked, her concern genuine.

"You're giving me a terrible headache. I have no idea what you're going on about. Colors, lights, techniques, and the different shades of blue. It's all just too much. *You're* too much!"

Vera smiled warmly at her new friend, unfazed and unoffended.

"So I've been told," she replied with a chuckle. "Mostly by my sister, but others have remarked the same," she clarified.

Mimi was unaccustomed to the woman's reaction. Normally, her abrupt and almost-rude tone kept people at a safe distance and allowed her space. People meant questions, and questions meant trouble. She only wanted to live as comfortably and as far from the meanness of her childhood as possible. The best way to ensure that life was safe was to live alone.

And yet, here was this young woman—elegantly dressed, exotic, and self-assured, who refused to be put off by Mimi's abrupt and rude responses. In fact, Vera seemed to find them amusing, and Mimi had no idea how to react. So, she didn't. She opted for no reaction at all in the hopes that her unwanted companion would find her dull and leave her for whatever elegant and refined home she had come from.

Vera watched as Mimi's suspicious nature dropped a veil over her features, shutting her down and closing off her Light. It broke her heart.

Patting Mimi's arm gently, Vera smiled at her new friend. If Vera decided she was friends with someone, it didn't matter what the other person thought.

"It's all a bit much. I know. Go home now and rest. I think you and I have a lot we can do for each other, but for now, maybe sleep is what you need," Vera suggested.

Mimi stood stone-faced as the young woman walked up to the corner of Royal and Canal Street and turned onto the bustling thoroughfare. Exhaustion overcame her as she made her way, alone, back down Royal toward the river that curved around the French Quarter like a lover, and home. The sun shone mercilessly down making a mockery of her lace parasol and causing her vision to blur with colors and flashes of light. Pigments hovered around the heads and shoulders of the people she passed. She noticed colors both striking and dull, opaque, and shimmering. If she paused to think about any one of them, thoughts came along with the color. The dark-skinned lady dressed in a maid's garb moved within a bubble of clear yellow, and Mimi thought of happiness, family, honesty, and joy. A small child stared longingly at a pile of hard candies displayed in a bucket that sat in the window of the pharmacy. The child stood among sparkles and flashes of bright pink and leaf green—a happy and well-loved soul.

Mimi walked through a confusing fog of colors until she reached the front door to her cottage. She dropped the pointless parasol and pushed open the tall shutters. She felt relief after making it home ahead of the obvious heat stroke that was fast approaching, and she adjusted to the cool dimness of the interior as her eyes fogged. The sight was bad, but it was the smell that caused her to swoon, something up until now she had only faked in order to pick a pocket or a vegetable cart. Sprawled across the small bed in the room adjoining her tiny front parlor lay Charlie, filthy and stinking of fish and old booze.

Mimi's legs collapsed beneath her, and she hit the bare wooden floor in a plume of skirts and petticoats. The sob that escaped her mouth roused the disheveled form of her father. He sat up and looked around in a blur of confusion and alcohol.

"Charlie! What are you doing here?" wailed Mimi in despair as she watched the pathetic man who she had hoped was gone forever heave himself to a precarious stance.

"I live here," he slurred, sounding befuddled and belligerent.

Mimi heaved herself up from the floorboards and stalked past the stinking man who invaded her newly-established sanctuary.

"No. No, you don't, Charlie. Not any longer!"

The stomping of her boot on the floor shook Charlie out of his muddled thoughts, and he looked at his daughter for the first time since her yelling roused him from his stupor.

"Weeeellll, looky here! Who's this all high an' mighty, then?" he slurred. His Irish brogue made his words swim together in a soupy mix of sharp R's and long E's.

Mimi watched her father take her measure from her straw boater wrapped with a wide black ribbon, her white shirtwaist and its belled sleeves, her plain blue skirt, and finally her black leather boots, stained and dusty from her walk through the muddy streets of the French Quarter.

"Been whoring yerself out, have ye now, girl?" asked Charlie slyly as he tried to rectify the shabby yet respectfully dressed young woman with the barefoot street urchin, he had left to her own devices years ago.

Mimi glared at the wreck of a man in front of her and snorted at the accusation. If he meant to insult her, he failed. If he were truly curious, she wouldn't give him the satisfaction of an answer. Charlie's hold on her comings and goings was forfeit when he abandoned her and left her to fend for herself.

"Get out," she spat at him.

"I won't," he spat back, the two standing off like street cats.

"Oh, you will, Charlie. You will leave this house this instant or—"

"Or what, girl? Or what? You'll kick your father out of his own house?"

"Yes! When I return, I expect you to be gone. I don't ever want to see you here again. Are we clear, Charlie?"

The once-handsome Irishman, known for his bright blue eyes and shining black hair, stared at the young woman who had been his daughter. His blue eyes, now cloudy with drink and illness, couldn't hold Mimi's and dropped to the floor. His shoulders dropped away from his collar and his scraggly gray hair that brushed the dirty fabric, and he stood defeated and broken.

Mimi turned on her toe and walked out the front door, leaving it open behind her. She had neither pity nor compassion for Charlie Blanchard and only wanted him gone for good by nightfall.

Chapter 16

The sun made its way to the western horizon, throwing the streets and alleys into shadows as Mimi returned to her cottage. When she had left Charlie there, swaying in his fog and funk of alcohol and filth, she honestly wasn't sure what she would do to back up her demand should he choose not to leave. The cottage, after all, was his. As far as she knew, anyway. Plans and counter plans ran in and out of her mind as she imagined scenarios where she would return and he had not left. Would she call the police? Would she bribe him to go? Could she make peace with Charlie living there again? Or would she, herself, flee the only home she had ever known? If so, where would she go? Perhaps a rooming house or one of the brothels. Could she set up camp on the levy behind the market? Absolutely none of these options seemed workable. Mimi dropped further into her dark thoughts as she made her way back home.

There was no light from the window, the front door's shutters were closed, and no smoke came from the small chimney. Hoping against hope that Charlie had fled—yet mentally gathering her strength if she were to find him passed out within the house—Mimi carefully climbed the three steps of her stoop and pushed in one shutter to peek quietly within.

All was dark and dim inside the cottage. While the lingering stench that hung around her father was still faintly detectable, his physical presence was gone. A sob escaped Mimi as she pushed the other shutter open and rushed inside to raise the sill of the

window, breathing in deeply the jasmine-
scented night air that flowed into her home.

"My home. Mine," she said aloud,
claiming the space as her own for the first
time.

Mimi stripped off her soiled blouse and
stepped out of her skirt. Her boots made a
dull *thunk* as she kicked one then the other
across the room where they struck the bottom
of the plaster wall and fell in a heap onto the
floor. She peeled the folded cash from the
sweaty fold of her elbow and unrolled her
stockings, dropping them next to her blouse
to soak and dry overnight. After draping her
skirt over the back of the wooden chair, she
stood, barefoot in her chemise, in the
gathering darkness of the evening. Mimi
heaved an exhausted, triumphant sigh. She
reflected on the successful pick that morning,
her encounter and possible friendship with
Vera, the bizarre realization that she could see

colors and feel the thoughts of the people around her, and finally finding Charlie in the house like a particularly unlucky penny. It had been a day that felt a month long.

Padding across the still-warm wooden planks, she closed the front door's shutters and lit the small kerosene lamp on the table. The theft from the businessman this morning had netted her at least fifteen dollars. Once added to her stash of cash, it might be enough to finally have a gas line in her cottage. She smiled while thinking about never having to light and trim the wick of the old kerosene lamp again and moved to the bedroom to add the stack of bills to the rest.

The rumpled bed still smelled enough of Charlie to make her wrinkle her nose in disgust. She was left with no choice but to strip the linens for washing in the morning. The thought of Charlie having been there all the while she was out that morning caused a jolt of panic to run from the roots of her hair to her bare toes. She crossed back into the common room and lifted the middle coffee can planter from the windowsill—the hiding place for her stolen savings.

Mimi almost cried. Counting the bills quickly, she saw that it was all still there. Charlie must have been too drunk to think of rummaging through the house, a surprise considering the obvious changes that had occurred since his initial departure.

Clutching the wad of cash and tapping one toe, Mimi looked around her three-room cottage with new eyes. The room in which she stood was the first room—the one she variously called the front or common room, parlor, or living room depending on her mood and designs for its future. The fireplace was against the wall facing the front door and serviced both the front room and the bedroom next to it. The small window to the right of the fireplace held her coffee cans of potted herbs. The bedroom contained the small bed with a window positioned over it and not much else; it was her least favorite space because it had been Charlie's domain when she was a child. The last room in the shotgun-style house was the kitchen which held the wood stove, another fireplace she used for heating her kettle, and a small table that held a wash basin used for both dishes and her personal toilet. The table and chairs used to reside in the kitchen, but Mimi had moved them to the front room. The lack of decor and furnishings didn't allow for much in the way of a hiding place for her money, so she considered the cottage's structure itself. The windows were bare of ornamental trim, and the decorative moldings at the floor and ceiling had long ago been stripped and sold by Charlie. The mirror that had been left on her stoop was the only framed item on her walls but had no backing in which she could stash money.

Mimi let out a puff of air in frustration and walked to the fireplace in the front room to light a small fire against the approaching night. Kneeling on the soapstone hearth, she pulled sticks and twigs from the pile of kindling stacked on the floor next to the fireplace. She dreamed of the day the kindling would be contained within a basket or bucket. But for now, it was a pile. One chunk of wood, slick with moisture that hadn't dried due to its place beneath the rest, slipped from her hands and landed with a *clank* onto the wooden planks next to the hearth. Mimi froze. A *clank*, not a *clunk*.

"That's odd," she said to the empty room and rapped her knuckles on the section of flooring that had made the metallic sound. Her rapping and knocking produced the same high-pitch sound. On either side of the space, it produced a lower, deeper noise.

The fire long forgotten, Mimi sat cross-legged and brushed dust and dirt from the floor and peered closely. Barely visible in the dark of the cottage were long scratches running against the wooden floor planks. She pried the edges up with her fingernails, and a small square of the floor lifted up and away from the surrounding boards leaving an opening that gaped darker than the darkening room in which she sat.

Mimi stood and brushed the dirt and debris from her underclothes. Barefoot, she padded over to the table to retrieve the oil lamp. Gooseflesh stood up on her bare arms, whether from the cool night air or discovering the space beneath her floor, she wasn't sure.

Holding the oil lamp over the hole in the floor showed that nothing was inside except for a few spiders that scuttled away from the unwelcome and unexpected light.

Mimi felt disappointed by the emptiness of the hidden space, though she wasn't sure what she should have expected. It was Charlie's house for so long; maybe it was a place to stash whiskey bottles. Although he never would have thought to hide them, so she guessed not. No matter the previous use of the hole in the floor, it was now Mimi's bank and safety deposit box. She couldn't afford for Charlie to make another surprise appearance and make off with her accumulating stash of money. Folding her stack of bills carefully, Mimi laid them in the hole and replaced the floorboards. She spread the dirt and dust of the hearth and kindling pile back over the space effectively hiding it from casual view again. She hoped, should her father pay another visit to the cottage, he wouldn't think to look for anything there — had he known about it to begin with.

"I'll need a basket and a small rug to properly hide the spot," Mimi explained to the potted Rosemary plant on the windowsill.

She felt pleased with her discovery and wondered what previous occupants had used the secret space below the floor for. She stripped the bed of the odious bedding, leaving it in a pile by the back door. The rain from the past few days had filled her makeshift bath and laundry tub and would allow her to soak the bedding and scrub it down with the bar of soap she had secreted from the kitchen at work.

Her toe struck something on her way back through the center bedroom. As she bent down to pick the object up, she was struck by chills that rolled up and down her body. Images flashed of Charlie as he stumbled down a lamp-lit alley, tears running down his face and his mouth open to emit a guttural cry of terror. The ominous *clip-clop, clip-clop* of something walking on two cloven hooves rang off the buildings on either side of Mimi's doomed father as he stumbled and fell. Mimi moaned and shook her head, trying desperately not to see or hear her father's plight.

Mimi remained crouched with Charlie's wallet in her hand and her eyes closed tightly. She was held captive by his last minutes of life. *Flash!* She saw Charlie try desperately to regain his footing, but he failed and fell back into the muddy puddles of the alley. *Flash!* A woman dressed in green velvet leaned over him from behind. Her grin was made malevolent by the sharp teeth protruding from her mouth. *Flash!* The woman rolled Charlie onto his back as easily as if he was an infant. She reached out to Charlie whose eyes had gone misty and dim; the struggle and fight were gone from him. *Flash!* Using one long fingernail, the monster in green velvet began to gouge bloody lines from Charlie's hairline down to his chest. *Flash!* The monster leaned down to lap the blood from Charlie's wounds. Again, again, and again.

Mimi cried out and dropped Charlie's wallet, and her eyes opened wide with panic and confusion.

"Oh, my god. Ohmygodohmygodohmygod," she babbled over and over again as she alternately paced the three rooms of her house and walked in ever smaller circles, only to begin pacing again. Her bare feet were numb from the damp and cold, and her arms chilled and dimpled with goosebumps.

As the sun rose over the slate-tiled rooftops and the kerosene lamp guttered and went out, Mimi sat slumped at her table, the wallet across from her.

She was exhausted, scared to death, and confused. But she knew one thing as sure as she knew her own name: Charlie Blanchard would never again return to the Saint Ann Cottage.

Chapter 17

His voyeuristic habits didn't bother him in the least. In fact, Bennette was quite proud of his skills with mirrors, utilizing them for travel and knowledge. The looking glass in Mimi's cottage allowed him to watch as the drunkard Charlie Blanchard stumbled into the cottage and collapsed on the bed in a funk of illness and alcohol. Bennette noticed that the aura of colors around Charlie was darkening. The already dull reds and browns signified the increased sickness and stress on his ill body and soul. While that was to be expected given the man's unhinged drinking and complete lack of nutrition, it was the green gashes that sparked through the aura that were of particular interest to the Mystic. The

Baobhan Sidhe had fed from Charlie, probably for quite some time. With prey easily available within the dark walkways and alleys of the French Quarter, Bennette believed that it had targeted Charlie specifically—he was, if even casually, a connection to its last human host, Mary.

One might be inclined to think the monk would be saddened by this conclusion; the pathetic life and times of Charlie Blanchard were even more desperate now. He was a walking food source for an evil being smuggled across the sea inside an unwilling human host. Quite the opposite was true. Bennette was beyond elated that the Baobhan Sidhe seemed attracted to Charlie due to his association with Mary. His entire plan relied on this assumption, and that meant Mimi would be of particular interest to the cloven-hooved entity.

Up until green sparks flickered through the sickly colors of Charlie's aura, Bennette was not completely sure the assumption he had based his loose plan on was true. Even more concerning, the monk didn't have an alternative idea for how to proceed if his assumptions were false. The French Quarter, as it moved into the 1900s, had a sick and drunk dockworker to thank for the eventual demise of at least one of the terrors that walked its streets. Or so Bennette dearly hoped.

Another of Brother Bennette's assumptions was that, due to her bloodline, Mimi would be a Seer in the way that her grandmother and mother were. Like his first assumption, it was borderline reckless—if he were wrong, more than a few lives would have been in jeopardy, though not his own.

"Ahhh, yes! I knew it! The Sight is strong enough to not need the opening song!

Imagine what you would be capable of should a woman of your line be available to fully open your eyes, Mimi!" exclaimed Bennette as he watched Mimi struggle with the visions of her father's death, produced by her touching his wallet.

As his unwitting protege cried out at the horrors that played behind her eyes, Bennette felt the stirrings of compassion not present since the loss of his Aisla. He knew that Mimi could be the best way to rid the physical world of the Dark Fae that was roaming unchecked through her neighborhood, but the cost would be high. For that, he was sorry.

Bennette shook himself out of the stickiness of emotion and reminded himself that he had already set in motion the events that would, most likely, spell the end of the vampiric Faerie. It would be far more dangerous to quit now than to follow the plan through to its conclusion.

Mimi watched the small brazier in the parlor's fireplace spring to life with the dancing gas flames provided by the new service she had finally saved enough to have installed. Still behind the times, many buildings and houses were now being fitted for electricity, Mimi was deliriously happy with this accomplishment. She even splurged to have a small brass lantern installed and connected for a perpetual flickering flame that illuminated her front stoop against the night's darkness. She had warmth and light available at her fingertips now, and this allowed her to finally acknowledge how much fear she had lived in for the entirety of her life thus far.

"No more," she spoke into the cozy front room. "Charlie is gone. Mam is gone. It's only me, and that makes it all a bit easier," she continued as she watered the bushy herbs on the windowsill and brushed the dust from her small table.

While she was finally safe enough to acknowledge the desperation of her life, isolation still seemed like a boon rather than a deficit. The danger of searching out a companion far outweighed the quietness of her cottage, so she continued in her solitary world.

Or, she would have, except Vera had not given up on Mimi. When Vera decided someone was her friend, the other person had very little to say in the matter, something Mimi was fast discovering.

It had been several months since their first meeting, and Mimi had grown tired of alternating between hiding and dodging Vera while out walking in the neighborhood. She struggled to come up with increasingly ludicrous excuses about why she wasn't available for a stroll or to sit for coffee when Vera inevitably caught up with her.

Vera was excited to talk to another person about the best pickpocket techniques and locations. She was equally excited to discuss the colors and thoughts that hovered around the public that both women observed. Mimi, however, found both topics to be intrusive and off-putting. She did her level best to avoid Vera completely.

It didn't work.

Mimi walked home in the gathering darkness after a particularly busy shift at the restaurant. She wanted nothing more than to enjoy the gas-lit interior of her home. Carnival season was in full swing, and the drunken revelry typically reserved for the patrons that came in after the normal dinner hours was now present from breakfast until closing. Carnival was a double-edged sword. There were marks for pickpocketing galore, both in the dining room and out in the streets, but Mimi was currently more likely to become a target herself. She didn't want to think about falling victim to thievery or strangers accosting her. Feeling hyper-alert for the better part of two months had left her exhausted. Perhaps exhaustion made her completely miss the clown that approached her from behind.

"Hey, darlin'! Happy Mardi Gras!" squeaked the grinning, oversized clown face that approached.

Mimi froze. Groups of rowdy and masked celebrants flowed past her on both sides, not one paying her the least bit of attention. Still unsure if the clown was a threat or simply a nuisance, she quickly crossed the street toward the safety of the gas lamp that threw the evening darkness into sharp relief.

"Mimi, wait! It's me, Vera!" called the masked figure as it eerily chased her across the street, narrowly avoiding an automobile that seemed to appear out of thin air.

"Vera!" exclaimed Mimi in annoyance. "What are you doing here?!"

"Here?" asked Vera, gesturing broadly at the circus atmosphere she clearly belonged in. "Or, *here*?" she queried, swirling one dainty gloved hand to show the small circle of light in which they both stood.

Mimi gave her a level stare and lit a Chesterfield King, blowing a series of smoke rings above her head. She was secretly pleased with this skill. While she masterfully formed the cloudy rings with an air of nonchalance, she had truthfully practiced for weeks in front of her mirror to perfect the trick—an activity Bennette had found highly amusing.

"Here," Mimi replied after a moment and used her lit cigarette to sketch a rough circle around the two of them.

"Oh, well. It's Mardi Gras, and you've been working non-stop. I thought you'd like to walk with me for a bit and see the costumes and parades," Vera suggested.

Swallowing the urge to ask how Vera knew her work schedule, Mimi looked at her companion and, for the first time, realized she might have a friend. The thought terrified her.

"Parades? I don't think there are any. Besides, I don't have a costume," replied Mimi. The excuse sounded pathetic even to her.

"I thought you might say that!" Vera laughed unperturbed and held up a length of golden cloth with two slits cut in it for eyes and sprays of sparkling gems glued about the length of it. It was hideous.

"Um, well, alright. Thank you."

She accepted the homemade mask and tied it around her head. She spread the eye slits into larger holes that she could actually see out of. At least she wouldn't accidentally walk into traffic and die, anyway.

Mimi felt Vera's delight as she put on the mask and watched her new friend's previous afternoon play out in her mind's eye: Vera cutting the golden cloth from the rearmaments of what used to be a tablecloth, cutting the eye slits with a set of ornate sewing scissors, and finally tacking the gaudy glass gems to the mask in an attempt to make it as festive as possible. Knowing that Vera had put in so much effort specifically for her warmed her heart a bit, and Mimi smiled in the direction of her clown-headed companion.

"Shall we go find some fun?" Vera asked enthusiastically, offering Mimi her arm.

The two young women wandered in and out of crowds and passed comments to each other about the color of this person or that, or a feeling, scene, or phrase that popped into their heads from a passer-by. They reached Canal Street and passed through the hundreds of spectators waiting for the marching bands and floats.

While Vera may have been aware of her gift for significantly longer, it was clear that Mimi was the stronger of the two. Working together, though, proved to be the most lucrative adventure. By the time they turned the corner at Bourbon Street and back into the French Quarter, they were thirty dollars and five gold pocket watches richer than when they had started their night.

Resting against the brick wall of a building shuttered tight for the night, the young women laughed and divided up their earnings, both flush with the fun and the success of the evening. Mimi, especially, was flying high on the newfound happiness of having a companion to share an evening.

As they started walking again, too agitated with the high of the night and the fear of being caught with the pile of cash and jewels, Vera's laughter died suddenly as she stopped and pointed, stuttering in alarm.

"What the hell is *that*?"

"What?" asked Mimi, on high alert now but not seeing what had so completely alarmed her new friend.

"Seriously, Mimi? You don't see them?"

"I only see a group of young men. Probably came in on the trains. They look rough, but we see that type all the time."

"Look again. I mean, really *look*," hissed Vera, giving the group of men a furtive sideways glance.

Mimi extracted a cigarette from the pack in her pocket with the ease of a chronic smoker. Never moving her eyes away from the end of the block, she struck a match, lit the roll of tobacco, and inhaled deeply.

Finally breaking her stare, she stood with her eyes closed for a minute or so. She exhaled the smoke, opened her eyes, and almost choked on her own exhaled smog.

"What the hell are those?!" she hissed at Vera who was still facing Mimi but casting furtive glances at the end of the block.

"I don't know! You see them now, though, right?"

"Yes, of course! But I don't understand. Are those men in masks?"

"I don't think so," replied Vera, shaking her head back and forth so hard that her clown head rattled hollowly on her shoulders.

"Well, they can't be alligators in clothing! That's simply absurd!" She tried hard to convince both Vera and herself.

"I don't know what they are. Alligators, lizards, who knows? But they are definitely not human! At least not to those of us who can *see* them!"

"We must not, for any reason, let them know that we can see them!" Mimi warned.

"Why?"

"I don't know! I really don't know, but I'm positive it would be a very bad thing if they could tell that we see them."

Vera took the cigarette from Mimi, inhaled deeply through the small hole at the grinning smile of her clown head, and dropped the smoldering butt to the pavement where she ground it out with one leather-clad toe. The display had the feel of a war general preparing to head into battle.

Mimi laid one hand on her arm, "Easy, Vera. All we need to do is continue walking like we were. Let's just pretend they are masked and turn the corner as soon as we've made it past, alright?"

Vera nodded, making the oversized clown head rattle again. Mimi stifled a semi-hysterical laugh at the absurdity of their situation. Linking arms with Vera, Mimi led her up the street, smiling and chatting inanely about absolutely nothing. The occasional snort of laughter escaped her mouth, figuring it would only add to the boozy picture they presented.

They reached the tight group of roughly-clad lizard-men. The men looked like what would happen if the bayou's alligators suddenly decided to ride the rails and disembark in the French Quarter—battered boots, smashed hats, torn suit coats, missing buttons, and stained with god-knows-what over trousers that had seen better years.

Mimi let her vision go soft and tried to call up information about the creatures through colors or images, but the only things she could make out were a swirling, twilight-hued lavender sky and the unearthly sound of hounds baying on scent.

The women walked on, putting one foot in front of the other, striding almost in tandem, and leaning perceptibly against each other. This was not an act. Each woman was so worried that the things in the ratty suits would know that they had been seen as their true selves that it was very difficult to not break out in a sprint.

Vera, inside her overwrought clown head, jumped in surprise at the sound of the lizard-men; their voices pierced through the background noises of Mardi Gras in the French Quarter. Her wide eyes met Mimi's.

The thought passed clearly between the two: *"They speak English!"*

Mimi and Vera cleared the group of scaly-skinned creatures and turned the corner, each letting out a breath of relief. They made it past unmolested.

Mimi leaned against a building, willing her legs to hold her upright. Vera finally pulled the ridiculous clown head off her shoulders and breathed in the night air. Her hair, normally curled perfectly, was plastered to her head in a mess of mats and tufts. Mimi chuckled at the sight.

Vera shot her a venomous look and dropped the clown head into the gutter.

"You can take the mask off now. I know you never really liked it," she muttered as she tried to use her fingers to tame the mess of black waves and disheveled curls that stuck up around her head like a deranged halo.

Mimi pulled the mask off, folded it carefully, and dropped it into her pocket. "I love it. And I love that you made it for me," she replied with an uncharacteristically warm smile.

Vera gave up on her hair, smiled, and kissed Mimi gently on the cheek, "Thank you."

They smiled at each other, flush with adventure, fear, companionship, and the glow of their stolen wealth. Mimi, for once in her life, felt happiness. Not just contentment, not just stability, but genuine happiness. Her eyes teared up from the enormity of the emotion when she saw Vera's back stiffen. The sound hit her like a blast of frigid air.

Clip-clop.

Clip-clop.

"Vera, we have to go. We have to go *now*," whispered Mimi, taking Vera's arm and dragging her across the street to where a streetlamp shone brilliantly.

"What's wrong? What is it?" whispered Vera, looking back and seeing nothing but a few masked, and entirely human, stragglers making their way back through the warren of streets to homes or rooming houses.

"I don't know what it is, exactly," whispered Mimi. Her eyes scanned the sidewalk across from them, "But it looks like a woman, walks on two hooves, has teeth like a snake, and it killed my parents."

Chapter 18

Mimi strolled down Royal Street looking for any 'help wanted' or 'hiring within' signs posted in the large windows of the upscale storefronts. Storyville, and the small businesses that had thrived amid its debauchery and revelry, closed due to the mounting pressure of reform groups, leaving her without a job. Mimi had squirreled away sufficient cash from her paycheck and pickpocketing to allow her to pay the gas bill and purchase food for a short time after becoming unemployed, but it wouldn't last for long. She would need another job and had, as of yet, not found anything that appealed to her, neither in aptitude nor pay scale.

Most restaurants within the French Quarter had been fully staffed for quite some time, leaving her the options of housekeeper, cook within a private residence or rooming house, or shop-girl in one of the storefronts along Canal Street. After working in the circus atmosphere of the café for so many years, she wasn't inclined to relive the chaos within the retail venue, and private homes simply didn't pay enough. Her skills as a pickpocket were exceptional but doing that full-time brought exceptional risks as well. There were always the possibilities of arrest and jail, physical assault by a mark that had caught on to her attempt at thievery, or conscription and forced labor by one of the organized groups operating within the French Quarter. Mimi preferred to work alone, only making the occasional exception to that rule when she and Vera paired up.

The gathering clouds were tinted purple and pink by the sun's setting rays, and Mimi hadn't noticed any signage to suggest her employment was needed. She sighed in resignation but wasn't surprised. This had been the case for the last few weeks. It had become her ritual to walk through the streets before she retired for the evening. The routine provided her day a structure that was lacking without a scheduled job to report to.

At the corner of Royal and Saint Ann, Mimi noticed a small sign that was newly hung from a darkened doorway, 'Fortunes.' That was it. It was hand-painted, simple, and shouldn't have been at all noticeable. But Mimi, who was out specifically to search for hand-lettered signs, spied it with ease. It wasn't a 'For Hire' sign, but she was intrigued and stepped inside the dimly lit room. The space was empty except for a round table covered in an elaborately fringed cloth, a hanging lamp, and two straight-backed chairs arranged to face each other across the table. In the center of the table sat a deck of cards adorned with colorful images, and Mimi gasped at the sparks of silver and gold, deep blue, and blazing red that jumped and danced around the deck.

Without a second thought, she snatched the cards from the table, tucked them into the deepest pocket of her skirt, and stepped quickly back out into the gathering twilight of the street. By the time the absent fortune teller returned to her shop, still smelling of the pipe that she had been smoking in the back courtyard, Mimi and the deck of tarot cards were several blocks away.

The gas lanterns that decorated the houses along her block danced in the darkening shadows, cheerful and bright. Mimi smiled with satisfaction, knowing her house was similarly lit. She marveled at how something as simple as having dependable light made her feel a part of her community; a legitimacy she felt her life with Charlie had been lacking. The irony that her light, and its symbol of a legitimate community member, had been purchased with at least fifty percent stolen cash was completely lost on the young woman. Mimi Blanchard, through no fault of her own, had morals and standards that walked a fine line between honor and survival.

Once safely inside her home, she sat at the table and shuffled through the deck of cards. She had seen her fair share of playing cards over the years. She had watched men in the parks of the French Quarter playing games of chance, and the gambling within the Storyville establishments were both legendary and notorious, but this didn't look like any deck she had ever seen before. First, the cards were quite large, easily double the size of standard playing cards. Secondly, the images were bright and with a variety of hues and pigments, not just the typical reds and blacks. The images were of people and items all in different states that evoked emotion and physical activity. She looked at a card that displayed the figure of a man lying in repose, with three swords arranged over him-it was difficult to tell if he was asleep or dead. As to what the card actually meant, Mimi had no clue. Other cards were similarly detailed but equally mysterious. She analyzed them for a moment. A woman, heavy with child, smiling invitingly from beneath a tree. A young man hanging upside down, one leg akimbo, arms held behind his back. The recurring image of a young man on a horse holding either a goblet, a staff, a sword, or a golden disk.

As she sipped at her tea and nibbled on an apple, Mimi separated the cards into piles. The cards that included a stick or staff were placed in one stack, any card with a golden disk went in another stack, and those with an image of a cup or goblet went into their own pile, leaving the cards with swords.

"Four sets of cards for each of these symbols," she mused aloud. "Goblets, sticks, disks, and swords. But what are you all?" she asked the remaining pile of cards that stared up at her.

"Twenty-two of you don't seem to fit with the others. Are you special, or are you not needed in whatever game is played with this deck?"

The cards remained mute, but Mimi began to feel the stirrings of something—a whisper and rustle of energy gathered behind her left shoulder.

"Who's there?" she asked, hoping her voice sounded firm and not as frightened as she felt. Being able to sense colors and images about the living had become second nature to her, but non-human interactions, such as the lizard-men of Mardi Gras or the ghosts and spirits that rose from the cracked pavements at dusk, still made her feel uncomfortable. While the spirits may have once been human, Mimi was not yet adept enough to tap into that vital part of them, making each seem alien and very much different from herself.

The gas flames crackling within the fireplace and the sounds of the street outside mingled together. The sounds of whispering and rustling behind her grew louder and more distinct. As the sun set and darkness reigned outside the small cottage, she could just begin to make out individual voices and dialects; a female voice sang softly in French, a throaty male voice droned on in a gravelly Italian, and the sing-song accent of the West Indies all spun together making the hairs on Mimi's arms stand straight up. Her eyes opened wide.

"Who are you? What do you want?" she demanded, not caring one bit now how scared her voice sounded.

The voices grew louder in response. She couldn't understand any individual words, though she was uncertain if that was the intention of the spirits or because she had only a passing knowledge of the languages they whispered, sang, and muttered behind her. Mimi felt cold and clammy.

Mimi's hands flew off the cards and covered her face—a purely infantile means of escaping something that frightened her, and she knew this. Rather than feeling embarrassed by the response that she was many years too old for, her fear escalated to terror as visions accompanied the voices. The first vision was of a small, dark-haired woman with alabaster skin. She wore a navy-blue gown that was over a century out of fashion, and she spun wildly from the end of a rope. Her face was swollen, and the hemp cut cruelly into her neck, but it was unable to stop the musical French she voiced as she swung and twirled like a horrifying marionette.

Next, Mimi saw a stout man sporting an elaborate silk and velvet coat that fell to his stockinged knees pace back and forth in front of a large paned window, gesticulating forcibly. His deep voice made the Italian words that spewed from his lips both deafening and threatening. In one hand, the gentleman held a small, polished stone. In the other hand, he clutched a deck of cards.

The last image settled around Mimi like a gentle wave of warm water, soothing and benign. The whispered lilting patois of Hispaniola settled at her left shoulder like a hug from a beloved friend. While Mimi still couldn't make out any words, the ebony-skinned woman who whispered to her radiated a loving strength that caused Mimi to let out a deep sigh. This last spectral being wore a colorful turban. Though her skin was unlined, her eyes held the wisdom of one who had entered the last years of life. The material of her dress was faded, shabby, and patched and fell several inches above her ankles, showing her feet to be bare. In one hand, she held a loosely woven rush basket full of sugar cane, and in the other, she held a machete.

Dropping her hands but keeping her eyes closed, Mimi whispered, "Who are you all? What do you want?"

A flash of blue and the hanged woman grinned and held up a feather. In heavily accented English, she said, "I will tell you of communications."

A flash of red and the wealthy Italian man held up the stone and the deck of playing cards and rumbled, "I will tell you of family connections and intrigue."

A flash of deepest black and the Haitian woman grinned at her. She held up a basket of sugar cane and said, "I will show you cycles—when to plant," with a flash of the sharp blade of her machete, "and when to bring in a harvest." Her smile was no longer warm or friendly. Gone was the initial warmth of the spirit who now frightened Mimi the most.

With her eyes screwed tightly shut, Mimi shook her head back and forth, back and forth. "I don't understand! What do you want from me? Why would you, any of you, send me messages of any sort?"

There was no verbal answer; all three spirits stood mute. Like a fluttering curtain coming down after Act One of the strangest play, banknotes of all nationalities, denominations, and styles fluttered down, down, down until the spirits were obliterated in the curtain of cash.

"Money?" asked Mimi in a small voice.

"Oh! That sounds like a grand plan!" a stray voice chimed.

Mimi jumped with a fright so complete that she was unsure which would happen first, soiling her underclothes or dying from a heart attack.

"Good Lord, Vera! What in the hell are you doing here?"

"I knocked and knocked, you didn't answer, so I peaked in. I thought you were asleep at the table until you spoke. What about money, now?" Vera grinned.

"I don't know!"

Mimi gestured with a sweep of her arm to the stacks of tarot cards on the table and explained, "I don't know what these are, what they mean, or why they seem to have ghosts attached to them…"

Vera watched as her friend trailed off, her voice high and scared.

"Well, they're tarot cards. Where did you get them?"

"Found them," Mimi muttered, looking at the cards as if they had turned into a pile of snakes writhing on her table.

"Hmm, yes. You found them," nodded Vera, knowing better than anyone how found items could wind up on a kitchen table in a house which was blocks away from where they had started.

Vera reached out to touch the closest card, the cloaked and hooded Hermit, and received such a jolt of energy that she yelped and pulled her hand back in surprise.

"Mimi! Where did you find these?"

"They were on a table in an empty shop. Their colors were so amazing that I pocketed them and immediately came home. Although, I think there's something wrong with them."

"You touched them? And nothing happened?"

"No, nothing. Not until I started separating them into these piles and wondering what their designs meant. Then they started talking," Mimi gestured vaguely over her left shoulder.

"*They.*"

Mimi watched the array of thoughts and emotions race across her friend's face. Had she done something wrong, aside from stealing the cards, of course?

"Should I take them back?"

Vera's laughter, genuine and delighted, bounced around the room.

"Oh no! Definitely not! They are most assuredly yours now. Their Guardians have welcomed you, if not *claimed* you. You know, I've heard of this type of thing, but it is rare. Most card readers are charlatans. Either the reader you took these cards from was as well and didn't know she had such powerful cards, or the Guardians of the cards have found you more to their liking. Either way, these cards are yours now."

Mimi set tea and some almost-stale cookies on the table while Vera rattled on about tarot cards, readers, and more. Mimi's head was spinning by the time she finished her tea and ate part of a cookie.

"Vera, please. I'm so tired—so very tired. I just need to find a job! The cards, their spirits, and their meanings are interesting. But unless they help me secure a job, it's just not what I need to concentrate on right now."

Vera grinned broadly, her white teeth sparkling against her cocoa-hued skin.

"Oh, darling! You don't understand at all, do you? You have just landed the most lucrative job you'll ever have!"

247

Chapter 19

Mimi had successfully presented the picture of a normal and legitimate member of her neighborhood, at least to any casual onlooker. Lace curtains now hung in the windows of the Saint Ann cottage, and the gas lantern at the front door flickered a lively dance in the purple nights the French Quarter was known for. If anyone cared to peek inside, they would see a scrubbed pine table with two matching chairs, a small sideboard holding a single set of homely Blue Willow China, an ornate glass cup, and a set of silver cutlery. A simple oval-framed mirror hung on the wall. In the next room was a well-made bed covered in a colorful quilt, adding to the general appearance of a simple, yet comfortable, home that was befitting for a single young woman of limited means.

A few details of the cottage were not evident to her neighbors. Hidden beneath the floorboards next to the fireplace's hearth were a deck of tarot cards, her late father's wallet, several gold pocket watches, and a stack of cash. When she left for the day, Mimi added her silver knife, fork, and the blue book that her mother brought over from Ireland. Though she rarely read the book, it made her feel better knowing if anyone should break into her house while she was out, the valuable silver and the only surviving items she had from her parents were safely hidden away. The tarot cards remained hidden, along with the cash and jewelry, to safeguard her sole means of making a living, her only means of paying the gas bill, and purchasing food. Mimi had never used a bank. Charlie and her mother never had either. No one had taught her how to open an account, and when she had briefly considered it, she realized that with no birth certificate or identification, she doubted it was possible anyway. She supposed that she could have asked Vera but never quite got around to it.

The sun shone through the lace curtains and left dappled patterns of brightness on the dark wood floors. Mimi carefully snipped the mature leaves and stems from her potted herbs. Though she didn't understand much of what was penned within the small blue book titled *Faerie Tales*, once she realized that her makeshift window garden was actually thriving, she consulted the family journal to identify the greenery that flourished in the coffee cans and examine what their uses were. The smell of mint swirled about the cottage as she snipped away at the bushy plant and tied the stems together, leaving a long tail of thread that allowed her to hang the bunch to dry. Consulting the sepia script on the page in front of her, she double-checked to make sure that the small bouquet of mint wasn't gathered too tightly at the stems.

She read aloud from the book, "Gather a handful of stems and good-sized leaves together in a loose bunch that will allow air to flow through and hang in a warm space with little moisture. Once dry, place the bunch in a brown paper packet to use as an infusion for an upset stomach and a mood lifter. Sweeten with honey if desired."

"An infusion must be a tea," she mused as she looped the long tail of thread over the curtain's rod and tied it securely. She added the mint to the line of other herbs she had cut and hung to dry: lavender, thyme, and parsley. The combined scent of the herbs, along with the mellow aroma of the sun-warmed wood floor, made her feel content and drowsy.

Flipping idly through the small book, Mimi wondered about the authors of the various entries and the book's notable lack of actual fairy tales. Based on the script, there had been at least two, and perhaps as many as four, people who contributed various recipes, rhymes, and planting suggestions. Holding her hand over the book, she tried once again to glean more information about her Mam's people, and once again she was disappointed.

Try as she might, she was unable to receive any clear images or information. Swirls of greens and browns spun around that flashed images of skirts spinning this way and that, as if twirling in a dance. Vague murmurings and bits of songs could just be made out, but with no distinct words or phrases, that offered Mimi no usable information. Every now and then, a blue-eyed face framed with dark hair would swim into view only to be replaced by another face so similar that it was difficult to tell whether it was the same person at a different stage of life or another woman entirely. Flashes of humble cottages, kitchen gardens, and huge bonfires came through on occasion. Once, the image of a young girl stumbling down a dirt road carrying a battered valise and a wooden box the size of a loaf of bread pierced through clear as anything she could see outside of her own window. But without context, Mimi was no further ahead of the meaning of the visions.

"Such nonsense combined with absolute practicality," she muttered, extracting a cigarette from the pack sitting next to the open book. She lit it with a piece of dried plant material that was set alight by a gas flame.

"Beware of mirrors and glass that show true, seal for safety with salt and rue."

Mimi blew three perfect smoke rings above her head and smiled. Were the women of her line superstitious or poets?

"'Good folk live within old oaks.' Who are *good folk*, I wonder, and why would they live in trees?"

Mimi opened the front door, tossed the end of her cigarette into the gutter, and looked up and down her street. The different verses and housekeeping tips from her family's homeland seemed completely out of place here in the bustling port city. Although, knowing she could make her own teas with her potted herbs was quite nice.

She stepped back inside and pulled the louvered doors closed. The puddles of sun had stretched out across the floor, suggesting it was well past two o'clock now. Setting the latch to secure the front door, Mimi walked through to her bedroom, stretched out on the bed, and pulled the quilt over her legs. She supposed she should have unlaced and removed her shoes, but she was already starting to drift off, her eyes heavy and her mouth slack.

The dream came again—revisiting the visions of Charlie's death. Over and over, she saw the pitiful figure of her father cower in the gutter, drunk and sick and dirty, as the woman with sharp teeth and nails gouged his skin and lapped up the blood. Over and over, the woman bent to imbibe in whatever vitality was left in the drunkard as his eyes unfocused and he stopped his feeble attempts at fighting back.

As the dream came to its inevitable conclusion, the gaslight showed Charlie Blanchard's lifeless form splayed on the dirty sidewalk, his skin sallow and yellowed, his eyes dull and clouded, and his teeth looking long and pointed as his anemic gums receded into his skull. While the original vision and its attending dreams showed no such images, Mimi knew with a grim certainty that the policeman who called for his corpse that morning wrote the death into the log as yet another victim of yellow fever that ravished the city. Mimi fretted and stirred as the dream kept its grip on her, holding her firmly within its gauzy embrace, yet just outside the realm of restful sleep. The quilt slipped to the floor as the young woman rolled to her side, whimpering with fear and dread she barely understood as the sound of hooves paced back and forth outside of the cottage's front door.

Clip-clop.

Clip-clop.

Clip-clop.

The dim shadows outside the bright circles of lamplight obscured the horror that paced back and forth in front of the shabby cottage in the middle of the block. To the casual observer, the lithe, red-haired woman—perhaps slightly overdressed in her heavy, dark green velvet dress—only appeared to be a lady out strolling before the sun set fully behind the horizon. The ominous sound of hooves was disguised excellently by the backdrop of horse-drawn carriages, gaudy automobiles, and neighbors calling to each other. However, if a passer-by were to stop and attempt to engage the redhead in conversation, the reality of the situation would be much different than an overdressed woman out strolling before dark. Her beautiful face, framed by flame-red hair, was marred by the long, pointed teeth of a predator. Heavy deer's hooves were found where pretty calfskin boots should be below the hem of the green velvet. The creature's smile was gleeful and deadly, and its eyes shone with a merciless delight. The Baobhan Sidhe had looked for weeks for Charlie Blanchard's girl, daughter to its former human host. It didn't particularly require a host, but the Faerie found that having a human was convenient and amusing, and the daughter of Mary appealed to her a great deal. At last, she found her and paced back and forth, deciding on the best way to take what it considered its own. If the mother had once been her vehicle, the daughter could be as well.

Chapter 20

Vera watched from a discreet distance as Mimi placed card after card between her and the client. She chose a location that was out of the way and under the spreading arms of an oak tree. The location was a quiet, private spot for conducting readings, and it offered a certain amount of security from the gangs that roamed the streets looking to rob vendors and pedestrians alike. Vera and Mimi looked down on these groups as base criminals. The irony was, in fact, lost on the young women.

While she couldn't hear what they said, the body language and colorful auras surrounding Mimi and the middle-aged businessman that sat across from her suggested he was receiving pleasant news.

Mimi was operating as both a skilled con woman and the very real psychic she was proving to be. The combination of these skills almost certainly ensured that no one left Mimi's readings disappointed or with extra coins in their pockets. Vera undertook the role of lookout, on alert for ruthless thieves that could potentially approach. She also functioned as security should one of Mimi's clients decide to turn the tables and rob her. And, if given the nod by her talented friend at the end of the session, she was to follow the client and relieve them of any extra cash or jewelry Mimi had noticed during their session.

The two young women had an elegantly elaborate ruse going, one that had netted each of them quite a bit of money. Mimi was never sure whether Vera actually needed the extra cash or if she was just in it for the fun. For Mimi, being able to buy nice clothes and enough food had become very dear to her after never having either before meeting Vera and acquiring the tarot cards.

The rotund, suit-clad gentleman stood up, handed Mimi a small stack of folded bills, tipped his hat, and walked away in the direction of the looming cathedral. Mimi gave the tiniest of nods as she gathered up her cards, and Vera ambled after the man, just a young woman out enjoying the afternoon before the skies threatened to open and dump inches of more rain onto the already sodden city.

As she closed in on her intended robbery victim, Vera noticed a group lounged along the edges of the building that sat at a ninety-degree angle from the cathedral's walls. There were at least a dozen of the lizard-men she and Mimi had last seen during Carnival. Other people walked by, seemingly unconcerned by the scaly-skinned men drinking from twists of brown paper bags—their suits dirty and stained, boots muddy and broken, and hats sitting akimbo on heads that held slanted, lidless eyes and slits of lipless mouths that stretched wide to display rows of dagger-sharp teeth.

To Vera, they were dramatically out of place, like a fantastical vision. She wondered if their inconspicuous nature meant that other people couldn't see them for what they truly were or if they couldn't see them at all.

As Vera watched the clutch of reptilian loiterers, a bosomy matron walked up to them, dropped a coin in front of a member of the group, and moved on quickly. Her social duty complete.

"Well, that answers that question," Vera muttered to herself. "They can be seen, but not like I see them."

"Aye, and it's best they never know that ye can see them," came a voice over her shoulder.

Vera jumped in surprise and spun around, nearly falling over in the process. The young man behind her, dressed in dated monk's robes, grasped her arm to keep her upright and marched her quickly past the lizard-men to the cavernous door of the cathedral just beyond.

"Wait, stop!" she hissed in annoyance as she yanked her arm out of the monk's grasp and stopped just inside the church.

"Who are you? How can you see them when no one else can?"

"I could ask the same thing of you, could I not?" came the gruff and rude response from the robed figure in front of her.

Vera steadied herself and squinted through the gloom at the stranger who had either accosted her or rescued her; she wasn't sure which.

He was younger than she had first thought, probably not much older than herself. His robe was made of rough wool, dyed a chestnut brown and cinched at the waist with a simple cord. He wore plain brown leather boots and no other adornments or jewelry.

"What did you see?" the monk asked quietly.

"I saw gators dressed as men," whispered Vera.

"I've seen them for a while now. Not all the time, just here and there. Sometimes there are only one or two, and sometimes they are in larger groups, like out there. Oh, my name is Bennette," he said in what he hoped was a friendly manner to the young woman in front of him. He very rarely interacted with anyone outside of his monastery, even less often with women, and he found himself feeling awkward and stilted.

"Nice to meet you, Bennette," replied Vera. "Should I call you *Brother* or *Father*?"

He stifled a sound of derision at either of those titles. Technically, he was still a Brother of his Order but in name only. He had wandered the In-Between for so long that when he did make a brief appearance at his monastery, he was left to his own devices within the kitchens or the library. Those who knew what he did had already taught him all that they knew of the Mysteries, and those who did not know never would.

"No, neither of those is necessary. Please, just Bennette."

"Fine, Bennette it is. I'm Vera," and she held her hand out for the young man to shake in a proper greeting.

Hesitating for just a moment, Bennette took Vera's proffered hand sheathed in pretty cotton lace.

Different images came into her mind fast and furious as Vera tried her best to remain upright. A flash of a pretty woman in a horse-drawn cart, her son sitting next to her. She was straight and proud. The boy was hunched and sad. The scene swirled slowly out of view and was replaced by a vision of the boy, now older, wearing robes and stepping through a polished bronze plate that reflected and sparked the candle flames set on the long wooden table behind him. Others who were dressed like the boy watched as he winked out of view. The next vision was Bennette leaving a small mirror on Mimi's stoop then quickly walking away.

Vera gasped as more visions spun into view and whirled away: Mimi walking barefoot as a small girl, stealing food from the market stalls. A woman—thin, sickly, and obviously related to Mimi—roaming the French Quarter, her eyes slanted and bottle green, her lips bloody and pulled back from sharp teeth. The same woman leaned over the prone form of an unknown man as she stood and wiped away the blood that ran down her chin. Her smile was wide and maliciously amused.

As Vera choked back a moan, the next vision showed the sickly woman, her brown eyes sunken, as she was led away by the grey-clothed Sisters to the hospital. Four starving and dirty children were hustled along, and not one noticed the wooden box the sick woman carried under her shawl.

"Oh, make it stop. Please, make it stop," moaned Vera as images of sick and dead bodies flashed by her fluttering eyelids.

The last vision was a beautiful redheaded woman clothed in a form-fitting green velvet gown. Her skin was alabaster porcelain, and her wide mouth and full lips grinned, showing long and deadly sharp teeth. The vision moved out as if it were viewed through a captain's spyglass, allowing Vera to see the being's entire figure. The last thing she saw before slipping completely into unconsciousness was that the redhead had hooves rather than feet.

Bennette caught Vera as she crumpled onto the marble floor, preventing her from banging her head painfully. He lowered her gently and adjusted her dress. If someone came in, he would claim that she had succumbed to the oppressive humidity of the day.

But no one came. Bennette patiently waited for her to recover, knowing the information he provided her was confusing, scattered, and distressing. She would need time to settle back into herself. He would allow her a few minutes but not much more than that. He needed Vera to understand, completely, what was happening and what he required of her. In his single-mindedness, it never occurred to the monk that Vera should have a choice in the matter.

Vera's eyes fluttered, opened fully, and struggled to focus. The monk swam into view, and the visions he had brought along with him came back in a tidal wave of terror and confusion.

"Who are you?" she demanded forcefully as she gathered her skirts and stood, refusing his offer of help.

"I told you, I'm Bennette."

"Bennette. I see," she spat back at him.

For a moment, they stood nose to nose. Neither uttered another word, a standoff of wills. Eventually, he broke the silence.

"As you can now see, there is much happening here that is dangerous and wrong."

Vera snorted, "It's New Orleans, 'dangerous and wrong' is the norm."

"This is not normal, and I think you are very much aware of that. Something was brought here that doesn't belong, and it will continue to wreak havoc until it achieves its ultimate goal."

"Are you talking about the lizard-men? What *is* their ultimate goal?"

Bennette shifted his weight from foot to foot, looking uncomfortable and embarrassed.

"What is it?" pressed Vera, narrowing her eyes at the monk who was obviously trying to evade the question.

"No, I'm not talking about the lizard-men. I'm not sure what they are or why they're here. I'm talking about the Baobhan Sidhe."

"The what?"

"The Baobhan Sidhe. It's the red-haired woman you saw in the visions I sent you. Except that it's not really a woman; it's a member of the Fae. A rare and deadly member of the Unseelie Court of the Fae.

"*You* sent me those horrifying visions?" she whispered in a furious spattering of words. "Why? Why would you do such a thing? And how did you know that I'm able to receive them? What is a Fae and the Unseelie Court? Who exactly are you, Bennette?" Her questions hit him like rapid-fire, a verbal assault that caused him to step back several feet in response.

"Stop."

His voice was commanding and cold and echoed throughout the marble-floored chamber. Vera blinked in surprise but closed her mouth with a jaw-jarring snap.

"The Fae are a race of beings that normally live in a world next to, but separate, from our own. They are not human. There are two tribes, or courts, the Seelie and the Unseelie. The Seelie are somewhat benevolent to humankind and strive for little to no contact. However, should contact be made, they are not normally antagonistic. The Unseelie Court dislikes humankind a great deal and will often hunt or actively attempt to interfere with men and women. Some are deadly, such as the Baobhan Sidhe. There are not many of them, thank the Lord, but the few that are alive are parasites and drink human blood. Most require a human host if they want to move too far afield from their homeland. This one, by contracting with a human, has managed to arrange for a proxy host of Scottish soil should its human host be unavailable. I showed you a vision of the dark-haired woman carrying the box; she was its unknowing host that brought the monster across the sea. Before that, there was another host. It is she that I will avenge."

Vera watched the monk as he rattled off most of the answers to her questions. At the end of his explanation, she noticed his face harden and his eyes gaze distantly as he mentioned avenging a woman from his past.

"So, this is personal to you, this blood-drinking thing?" she asked.

"Aye. It killed someone I loved a great deal. Used her, sucked her body dry of all vitality, then fled to another host body to continue its disgraceful feeding. Once that body was destroyed, it was left to wander this city, attacking and drinking from any unsuspecting ne'er-do-well it happened to come across. If that human is lucky, the Fae will kill him outright, drinking his blood until not one drop remains to keep him alive. If unlucky, the demon will play with the human like a cat with a mouse, drinking little bits here and there. Amusing itself by hunting and stalking him until fear and madness take over, and he all but welcomes death at the hands of the Fae."

Vera stood still and watched the monk's face as fear, anger, sadness, and determination all vied for dominance.

When he had steadied himself, she asked quietly, "I see how this is personal for you, but why involve me? Why should I become a part of this deadly thing you have going with something that is not even human?"

"Because you've already encountered it. It already knows you, and it has its sights set on Mimi for its next host," he warned.

Bennette stepped back across the marble floor, his boots ringing out loudly within the empty expanse, and gently took Vera's hand once again. She closed her eyes and let the visions wash over her, not fighting them this time. Mardi Gras night where she and Mimi had first encountered the lizard-men, the terrible mask she had made for Mimi to wear, pickpocketing unsuspecting revelers, and just as they were sure they had made it safely past the scaled vagrants, the sound of hooves on bricks. Slow, steady, and deadly.

"Mimi said that whatever was there had killed her father," Vera whispered.

"Aye. And her mother who was the host who brought it across the ocean, though Mimi doesn't know that."

Vera nodded her head, not in understanding but in agreement, "I'll do what you need if it will keep Mimi safe."

Bennette regarded the pretty young woman standing across from him and thought it was odd she felt it was her place to agree or that the end goal was to keep Mimi safe. As far as Bennette was concerned, Vera would do what was needed because it was needed. The goal was to stop the Baobhan Sidhe, not assure Mimi's safety. Of course, if Mimi made it safely out of this, all the better. But it wasn't a foregone conclusion of the monk's plans.

Chapter 21

Vera let Mimi's throaty voice wash over her and float through her consciousness as her own thoughts focused on her first meeting with the monk called Bennette almost a decade ago. As life within the French Quarter flowed alongside world events like the Great War and the resulting party that would become known as the Roaring Twenties, it was easy to relegate the visions of a blood-sucking entity to the farthest reaches of her mind. If the images escaped her, she would disregard them as the ravings of a mentally disturbed clergyman. Vera had perfected the ability to tune out things that were disturbing or upsetting. But the monk was persistent and had taken to finding her when she walked the streets of the Quarter or sent terrifying images to her as she slept. He ensured she would never stray too far from the path he had set her upon. Throughout the previous years, she had managed to avoid stepping too far outside of her comfortable life. But, with the end of the party and the beginning of the austerity that resulted in the stock market's collapse, Bennette had stepped up his game. His insistence on Vera fulfilling her promise had bordered on stalking. If she slept, she dreamed visions sent by Bennette. If she took a stroll without Mimi, within a block or two the monk took a place beside her, matching her step for step. He never spoke a word and rarely looked at her directly, but his continual presence had become foreboding.

"Vera, hey! Have you heard a single thing I've said?" Mimi's deep voice displayed signs of annoyance and hurt feelings.

Vera snapped her attention back to the woman sitting across the table from her. "I'm so sorry! Yes, I've been listening. I promise."

"Liar," replied Mimi, popping the last powdered sugar beignet into her mouth and dabbing at the front of her blouse with a napkin.

"Don't be angry with me," sighed Vera. "I haven't slept well in just about forever."

"How come?" asked Mimi, sipping at the café au lait that was just as much a part of Café Du Monde as the sugar-laden fried dough the coffee house was famous for serving.

"I don't know, just haven't."

While Bennette had never specifically asked her to not tell Mimi about their meeting, it seemed fairly certain the monk expected their partnership to remain a secret. It took all of Vera's considerable strength not to roll her eyes at the word her brain provided—partnership—ha! She was more like a hostage to Bennette and his plans, but she didn't know what to do about it. The fact that Mimi remained safe seemed to allude to the possibility that Bennette was simply insane. But the consistent attacks and dead bodies that all had signs of sallow skin, deep scratches, loss of blood, and elongated teeth offered the terrifying alternative that was not only sane but correct. Vera would err on the side of caution to keep her dear friend and years-long companion safe. She would remain a hostage for that.

"I've gotten pretty good with the old recipes in my Mam's book. Maybe a tea would help you?"

Vera smiled. Mimi's use of 'Mam' and her concern for Vera's wellbeing never ceased to warm her heart. Mimi was an intimidating woman with a cigarette-scarred voice and the cut-throat attitude of a street urchin showing through her stylish clothes and coiffed hair, but her heart was big, and it was bright for Vera.

"I think I would like that, thank you. At this point, I'm desperate for a good night's sleep."

Mimi and Vera, companions for over twenty years now, strolled leisurely through the streets that made up their neighborhood. The bohemian elements that had taken over and defined the atmosphere of the French Quarter in the 1920s hadn't completely fled with the end of the boozy, jazz-filled party, but it had quieted down significantly. The effects of the Great Depression could be seen in the groups of men loitering along the street or on corners asking for day work or a coin and in the uptick of barefoot, sunken-faced children that roamed in gangs throughout the markets and alleys.

"I want to gather them all together and feed them," Mimi whispered as they approached a group of children. Some of the children danced and some used sticks against the metal lamppost to bang out a rough jazz beat, hawking money from anyone who passed by their makeshift band. Vera smiled as her friend dropped several coins onto the rag that may have once been a shirt spread out in front of the drumming and dancing group of children. The rag was almost devoid of money but whether that was from a lack of donations or because the children were savvy enough not to leave it all out was anyone's guess.

Linking her arm through Vera's, Mimi blinked away tears and noted where the group congregated. Later on, she would return on her own to see where the children bedded down for the night. She added them to her list of children that would wake in the morning to an orange, some shoes, or a clean sweater next to their makeshift beds in doorways and beneath park benches. Mimi was tough but would never forget how it felt to be alone, cold, and hungry while growing up. If she could relieve another child of that horror, she would do so.

"When do we read again?" Vera asked as they rounded the corner and made their way down Saint Ann to Mimi's cottage. Over the years, Mimi had seen Vera's home a few times, a palatial townhouse several blocks from the small shotgun. But, by an unspoken agreement, the women kept to the cozy privacy of Mimi's cottage.

"Whenever you'd like. The newspaper ads have done nothing but cost money. It seems to work better if I just sit in the square and wait for someone to approach."

"Well, let's at least have a sign to attract customers," Vera replied, disappointed that the newspaper ad hadn't panned out. It added an air of legitimacy to their racket that she found appealing.

"Sure, whatever you'd like," mumbled Mimi. Her mind was still on the gaggle of urchins they had just left. There were five of them, so she would need to add more fruit and clothing to her list of things to gather the next time she went shopping. *Shopping.* It was a miracle she could think of shopping so easily now—a miracle she hoped would never leave.

"Thank you," Mimi whispered and leaned over to kiss Vera on the cheek.

"For what?"

"For making all of this possible. I owe you everything." She spoke with intensity and caused Vera to stop walking.

"What's going on? Why the sudden gushing of love and gratitude?"

"Just those kids and realizing that I can help them feel a little bit of comfort now, and that is because of us."

"Don't be silly. You would have been just fine without me," Vera said breezily, carefully hiding her discomfort. Because of the visions, she knew more about her friend's early life than Mimi had shared, and she felt guilty for the knowledge.

Sensing that this was the end of the discussion, the women resumed their walk, arms linked. Mimi was still amazed she could, on a whim, purchase an orange, let alone a half dozen of them and a pair of children's shoes.

As the sun fell below the horizon and the gas streetlamps disrupted the shadows, Mimi and Vera settled at the small table in Mimi's cottage and perused the blue book filled with herbal remedies and folklore.

"It says here that Valerian root tea can help you to sleep but it tastes pretty awful. Maybe it will go down easier if I add some mint?"

Hearing no response, Mimi looked up from the book and saw that Vera had drifted off, seemingly lost in her thoughts.

"Vera! Mint! Do you like mint?" hissed Mimi in exasperation.

"What? Oh, yes. Mint is lovely, thank you," Vera said weakly. Her gaze was somewhere to the left of the conversation.

"Really! I've grown tired of talking to myself today. I think I'll make tea for you tomorrow."

"Yes, OK. Very good. I'll stop back then," Vera agreed as she gathered her sweater and left Mimi's house with not much more than a small wave over her shoulder. Mimi stared after her, unsure whether she should be concerned or thoroughly annoyed.

Vera walked through Saint Ann Street, down Royal, and up to her own house. In her head, she replayed the events from Mimi's cottage that only she was aware of. The mirror on the wall, left by Bennette so many years ago, had come to life as Mimi read on and on about this herb or that. The mirror showed hellish visions of the poor souls attacked under purple skies throughout the French Quarter. Drunken businessmen and indigent street people alike were pursued by the red-haired thing that stalks its prey deliberately and slowly, knowing that it would eventually run its prey to the ground and feed at its leisure. The attacks were masked by the dreaded fevers that cropped up every few months, but they still provided lurid fodder for the local myths of vampires that stalked the night-darkened streets. Mimi didn't see this display of horror and gore because her back was to the looking glass. Had Vera not been so shocked at the terrifying images displayed, her face may have shown something was amiss. As it were, the shock on her face only showed as distraction and weariness, leaving Mimi irritated rather than horrified.

Vera entered the tall double doors and dropped her sweater onto the dainty French antique chair in the entry with the carelessness of someone who knew that someone else would be around to retrieve it, clean it, and replace it within her wardrobe. Climbing the stairs to her rooms, she felt the safety and security of her family's wealth and stability settle around her like a velvet mantel. The shock that left her feeling as if she had floated several feet above her own body flew off like an ill wind and left her astonishingly angry at the coldness of Bennette's delivery and the inescapable road ahead of her.

She could tell by the surroundings and dress of the victims in the mirror that some were from Mimi's childhood, a few from the present, and there were some shown far into the future. Being able to look at clothing and buildings from a world fifty years in the future would have been incredibly interesting had it not been for the vein of sameness running through each vignette—children and adults hunted, fed from, and left like so much trash in the gutters of the French Quarter. Bennette's message was loud and clear; her time to evade and ignore their agreement had passed.

The Mirror Dance: A French Quarter Faerie Tale

Chapter 22

Vera sat cross-legged in front of the mirrored armoire door. Her linen pants would surely be a wrinkled mess by the time she stood back up, but it didn't much matter to her. With the passing of her parents and her sister married and gone up north to live, the large townhouse was occupied only by herself and the few staff that were required for the home's daily upkeep. Her penchant for wearing trousers rather than dresses was fully enjoyed within the sanctuary of her own four walls. Even as a woman of means aged well past thirty, societal demands still weighed heavily outside her front door.

For most of the summer, Vera had alternated between grudgingly engaging with

Bennette and actively avoiding him. When she was with Mimi, she absolutely avoided the monk and his passive-aggressive messages and signs. To acknowledge them would put her at risk of having to answer questions from Mimi, and Vera dearly hoped to avoid that.

As the summer heat and its oppressiveness gave way to October's temperate breezes, Vera had enough of the cat and mouse game she and Bennette had played for so long. She wasn't getting any younger, and Mimi was older yet. The situation needed to reach its conclusion.

Over the years, Vera had seen enough of the monk's visions to understand that he traveled by way of mirrors. While she had known for quite some time it would come to this, she was now ready to use this knowledge to contact Bennette. After all of these years, she had never done so. The monk was intimidating and abrupt, and he had a history of being rude—attributes that left Vera feeling a bit off kilter. As street smart as she was, remnants of childhood lessons still dictated that clergymen were obeyed without question.

Vera straightened her head scarf, adjusted her left leg that was falling asleep, and squared her shoulders. Taking a deep breath, she settled herself and stretched both arms out so that her palms rested on the mirror's surface. She breathed in deeply one more time, closed her eyes, and opened herself to whatever visions would come. Images she had seen before slipped past, showing Bennette in various times and locations. When she finally saw him as she knew him, walking within the French Quarter during her own time, she held onto those images and called out to him in as commanding a voice as she could muster.

"Bennette! Brother, priest, monk, or witch, I call to your spirit and demand that you appear!"

The silence in the large home loomed heavily while Vera waited for a response. Beyond her window, three stories down, she heard cars rumbling and rattling on the street and the shouts of pedestrians narrowly escaping the cavalier drivers of the hulking steel automobiles.

"Bennette! I call to you and command you—come to me!"

Goosebumps rolled from the center of Vera's shoulder blades to the very top of her scalp and back again. The air became incredibly dense and heavy as if a summer storm approached. Vera felt her hair raise at the roots; her scarf was the only thing that kept it from standing on end. Bennette's anger was palpable. She knew that if she had an ounce of sense, she would feel terrified. But she was exceptionally tired, and that resulted in a focus so determined that it was impenetrable. The years of back-and-forth engagement and hiding, terror, sleeplessness, and worry had left her hollow. There was no room left for anything except the rock-solid desire to finish this task.

Vera opened her eyes and dropped her arms, aching from having held them at shoulder level for so long, and watched the glass. The monk's anger flowed about the room like a hunting cat, heavy, foreboding, and deadly. She shook off the heaviness that attempted to thwart her call. Vera recognized a man's bluff when she saw, or felt, one. Bennette may not like having the tables turned on him, but his temper tantrum wouldn't stop her. This grand scheme was his, and he had dropped her into the middle of it without even asking her thoughts on the matter. He may be a monk, he may be a priest, he may even be a witch, but he was still a man, and Vera had no time or patience for machismo.

Still watching the glass, Vera lit a cigarette and stretched her legs out, crossing one laced spectator over the other, and waited. As the energy in the room dissipated and settled in the corners, the mirror clouded. Silvery-grey wisps swirled and twirled within the frame. Tiny sparks of green and brown bloomed here and there as the opaque mists danced.

Vera blew a long stream of cigarette smoke into the gathering mists, hoping Bennette could see her and recognize the action for the insult it was.

"Don't be rude, Vera."

The deep Scottish brogue came from behind, making Vera jump to her feet. The ash that fell from her cigarette dropped onto the crimson Persian rug and burned a small hole in the wool. Vera stubbed it out with her toe as she looked at the robed man who stood in the doorway.

"What the hell, Bennette?"

"There are many mirrors in this house. I can come and go from whichever I choose as long as it's not been warded. Seeing as you don't know how to do that, I had quite a few options at my disposal to answer your... *call.*"

Vera's face flushed with heated anger and embarrassment. The damnable man had called her bluff and was now smirking at her. She would have liked nothing more than to stride right over to him and kick him squarely in his robe-draped shins. The mental image she conjured made her smile, and she used it. Grinning at the monk, she settled her shoulders and met his gaze.

"Clever."

"Aye. What can I do for ye, then?"

Based on his heavy brogue, it was obvious that Bennette was deeply angry at her for summoning him, and Vera was happy about it. She had been at his beck and call for years; it felt good to be the one beckoning for once.

"We need to end this. How many years has it been since you demanded my help with your, er, *problem*? We're no further ahead, and I am tired to my bones. I need to sleep, and I need Mimi to be safe. That means you and I need to finish what you started god knows how long ago. Really, Bennette, how old are you, exactly?"

"You've been avoiding your duty—not I. I've provided you with all the information you needed to do as I asked of you, and yet you've evaded me. As for my age, that is relative. I am both older than you could possibly imagine and younger than you currently are."

Vera's mouth gaped slightly, simultaneously offended and confused.

"My duty? Seriously? My duty? You have a very strange idea of duty. Be that as it may, you said doing as you asked would keep Mimi safe. I'll follow through with *my duty*, but only for her. And that bit about your age, really? Do you say these things simply to try my patience?"

"No, *you* said it would keep Mimi safe. I did not," corrected Bennette quietly as Vera turned to light another cigarette, not hearing his clarification.

Vera blew a stream of grey smoke at the ceiling, ignoring the disapproving look from the monk.

"Alight. We agree to finish this, yes?"

"Aye. It is past time to finish this," he agreed.

Bennette followed Vera down the staircase and into the front parlor, seating himself on a silk-clad loveseat across from the Louis XIV chair Vera chose. The grandeur of the room bored him. Bennette had seen many rooms like this one, many different times.

A dark-skinned woman with an ample bosom appeared with a tray of cold drinks, sugared fruits, sliced cheeses, and French bread. The older woman, wearing a simple dress with sensible shoes, placed the tray on the small table between Bennette and Vera. She gave her mistress's choice of clothing a disapproving glance and moved off into the cavernous reception hall, further into the depths of the house, and presumably to the kitchen.

"I'm not sure what we have to discuss. You've known all along what needs to be done," Bennette said after a moment.

Vera picked up a glass of cold tea and handed it to her guest who accepted it gratefully.

Sipping on her own tea, she watched the monk over the rim of the sweating glass. She decided to let him speak as long as he wanted as she collected her thoughts. Her tenuous hold on her position needed to be maintained, if only for her ego's sake.

"You must find the box containing the Fae's homeland soil and destroy it. As long as that exists, it can wander at will with no need for a human host."

"OK. And what happens after I do this? Does this Fae just, *poof*, disappear? Does it simply fade into the nearest mirror as you do?

What becomes of it once the box is destroyed?" she asked.

Bennette began to fidget uncomfortably, and Vera watched with growing alarm.

"You don't actually know, do you?"

"Aye, I am almost practically certain that without the box as a refuge, the Faerie will die."

"'*Almost, practically certain?*' Bennette! That is not knowing, that is assuming! All this time and you're not sure how this works?"

Bennette stared over Vera's shoulder at the wall of portraits behind her. He glanced over a gallery of her relatives, all with Vera's wide, almond-shaped eyes, sleek black hair, and café au lait skin.

"There's no way to be certain," he whispered. "The Old Ones never knew of a human that had compacted with a Baobhan

Sidhe, so there are no written accounts or instructions on how to handle it. I've been reading and praying, and the most logical way of destroying it is to destroy the box," he explained, hunched in his seat.

Vera stared at the monk.

As the grandfather clock ticked away the minutes and their cold tea warmed to room temperature, they sat in silence, each lost in their thoughts.

When the maid entered the room to remove the untouched tray of food and swap the warm tea with cold replacements, Vera shook herself from her thoughts.

"Bennette, how often does the Baobhan Sidhe return to this box?" she asked.

"When the moon is new, the demon returns to its box. Why do ye ask?"

"I think that may be the secret. Destroy the box when the Faerie is inside of it so it can't find a host to live in. Do you see?"

He thought for a moment and agreed, "Aye, I do. Why did I not think of it before?"

Vera shrugged. She wondered the same thing but said nothing.

"When is the next new moon?" asked Bennette, still mentally kicking himself for missing something so incredibly obvious for all this time.

"Really? The all-seeing, all-powerful, time-walking priest doesn't know when the next new moon is?" she teased.

Bennette glared at Vera, her jeering hit home with a painful clenching of his chest.

"I am not 'all-powerful' nor am I 'all-seeing.' I see *many* probabilities, and I can help those probabilities turn into realities. My power rests in manipulating the possibilities to accomplish a future goal. I would think you would have known this. Otherwise, I would have been able to do what I asked you to do by myself and skip this ridiculous small talk and wasted time."

Vera blinked rapidly as her brain grabbed his words and attempted to process their meaning.

"By 'manipulating possibilities' you mean manipulating people, don't you? Manipulating ME?"

"I think you should take a breath and think about this, Vera. You and Mimi have made a living by manipulating people, and you sit there and judge me? At least what I'm doing is out of love and not for coins."

"How dare you," she hissed. "Do you think I've not done everything I've done for love, including this so-called deal with you?

Everything I've done since I met her, Bennette, has been for love."

Bennette watched the woman across from him choke back tears of rage, hurt, fear, and frustration. He finally saw what he had missed all these years. The devil-may-care women, no longer young, could have gone anywhere, married well, had children. She had turned her back on all of that. Love, indeed.

"I apologize, Vera. I have committed a grave offense in assuming that my love is somehow greater than another's."

Vera blinked back the tears that she refused to let fall in front of the arrogant man and lit a cigarette.

"Accepted. The new moon is in three weeks. Let's finish this before Christmas, Bennette. I'm tired."

Chapter 23

Vera couldn't believe it; everything had all happened so quickly. She had always heard that one's life passed before their eyes when they died, but for her, it was simply the hours leading up to it, just a normal late-October afternoon that started like so many others.

"Take your sweater, Dear. It's chilly in the shade."

Mimi rolled her eyes at the instruction, finding it amusing that the overtly parental instructions were coming from someone several years younger than herself.

"Vera, it's really not that cold out. I have long sleeves on. I should be fine," she protested.

Pretending that she didn't hear her, Vera chose a light blue cardigan with embroidered daisies along the collar and handed it to Mimi.

"Here, this one will be lovely with your dress."

Mimi smiled to herself, grabbed her pocketbook with its small amount of cash and her tarot cards inside, and pulled the front door closed behind her. Vera stood on the sidewalk, eying the brilliant blue sky.

"Do you think it will rain while we're out?" Vera asked as they walked down to Royal Street.

"Goodness! Could you find one more non-issue to worry about today?" laughed Mimi. "There is not a single cloud in the sky!"

"I just feel like something is off, or perhaps I'm forgetting something," she muttered. Her brow furrowed as she thought back from the time she left her home until now, unable to put her finger on whatever was nagging at her.

"You're still not sleeping, are you?" Mimi asked as they stepped around a large pile of household garbage that someone had rudely left in the middle of the walkway.

"It's getting better, really," assured Vera, wrinkling her nose at the odious pile of refuse. "Why do people do that?" she asked, not expecting an answer.

"It is getting worse and worse lately," agreed Mimi. "Vagrants, bums, piles of garbage. Why, yesterday I saw a man rob another one at just after ten o'clock in the morning!"

"Awful," agreed Vera. "I miss the way things were before so many lost their homes and jobs. It's supposed to be getting better, but for those who fell hard, I don't think there's much of a chance of getting back up."

The women stepped around a mound of dirty rags that barely covered an even dirtier man curled up on a square of cardboard.

"Is he asleep, you think?"

"Asleep or passed out," replied Vera, her voice containing equal parts sympathy and disdain.

Mimi stopped after several feet and turned around to face the pile of dirty rags. She breathed deeply and looked at a point just past the lump that might be the man's head. After a few seconds, a wash of dingy colors undulated, olive green, dark brown, and black shot through with red, and grey.

"He's alive but very sick," whispered Mimi.

"You don't need the Sight to tell you that," and Vera steered Mimi away from the lump of rags. "We need to get to the square. I think it will be a good day for tourists."

Taking a deep, hitching breath, Mimi allowed herself to be guided away from the vagrant. She knew there was nothing she could do to help him, but men in that state would forever remind her of Charlie, and it broke her heart. It may or may not be a blessing that this man was alive, but Mimi would leave that to him and whatever gods watch over drunk men.

Crossing Royal and walking down the alley, the two women passed the church on their left with the square opening in front of them. Vera was right. Men and women strolled hand in hand as smaller versions of them ran circles around the benches and plants that made up the structure of the park.

Mimi and Vera found an unoccupied bench and sat down facing away from the church and scanned the pedestrians that wandered past enjoying the sunshine and relative coolness of the day. Not one realized the two smartly dressed ladies watching the crowds were gathering all the information necessary to either pick a pocket or solicit a tarot card reading. While a reading was truthfully the real deal, it was also a route to ultimately losing a watch, wallet, or ring.

"There, look," said Vera, tipping her chin toward a bespectacled gentleman who approached their bench from the corner of Chartres Street.

"What do you see?" Mimi asked, holding a small compact to her face, ostensibly fixing her lipstick.

"A bright green aura flecked with blue and sparkles of gold. He's healthy, prosperous, and not an angry sort. I say we hit him."

"Done," smiled Mimi.

Vera stood up from the bench, picked up her pocketbook, and ambled slowly in the direction of her mark. She allowed him to close the gap by fiddling with her purse and straightening the waist of her skirt. Still looking down, she started to walk, moving directly into the unassuming gentleman who was about to feel terrible for knocking over such a sweet lady.

"Oh! Oh, my goodness! Miss, I am so sorry!" blubbered the man, his glasses slipping down his nose as he bent to help Vera up from the flagstones.

"Oh, gosh, what's happened?" breathed Vera in a small, girlish voice, not at all like her own.

"Miss, I'm terribly sorry. I didn't see you at all! Are you hurt?"

She blinked prettily at the man clutching her elbow then buckled her knees in an impressive portrayal of an old-fashioned swoon.

Mimi watched with a grin she could barely contain as the would-be gallant gentleman stepped into the space between himself and Vera, allowing her full access to his front suit pocket.

The deed was done when Vera miraculously came to, fanning herself and smiling prettily.

"I'm fine, sir. I promise. Just a bit of dizziness from the sun. Thank you so much for your help! No, no, I am really just fine. I'll go sit down on one of those benches for a few minutes. Don't you worry a bit!" assured Vera, waving off additional offers of help.

The man eyed her uncertainly, feeling he would be remiss in his duty if he didn't at least help Vera to a bench.

Wondering how they were going to get rid of her rescuer, both Vera and Mimi smiled in relief when the man's wife hurried out of the cathedral to join him. Vera waved daintily at him as he walked past her bench, the picture of feminine health.

Mimi watched as the couple made their way out of the park and onto Decatur Street. Once the couple was gone, she jumped up and grabbed Vera's arm, hauling her off the bench. The women ran back into the ally from where they had originally entered the square.

"Oh! I didn't think you'd be able to lose your knight in shining armor," Mimi laughed as they leaned against a brick wall, now out of sight from the people wandering through Jackson Square.

"I know! Oh, my, it was nice to find a gentleman, but goodness! What a sweetly, silly man he was!"

"What were you able to get before you were overcome with the sunlight?" she laughed at Vera's charade. It never failed to work on a gentleman mark, and it never failed to amuse Mimi.

Vera reached into a deep pocket on the side of her smartly tailored skirt and pulled out a thick wallet as well as a gold wristwatch.

"Oh! You got both? Very good!" Mimi cried with delight.

Vera opened the calfskin wallet and flipped through the folded bills. "It looks like there's close to—" Her eyes opened wide, and her mouth made a small O shape as her knees buckled in a cruel parody of her earlier performance.

Mimi stood stunned, not understanding what had just happened.

Vera collapsed, falling onto the dirty pavement and dropping the wallet and watch on her way down. As the young man wiped the blood from his knife's blade, scooped up the wallet and watch, and walked without a care in the world into Jackson Square, Mimi finally moved and dropped to her knees beside her friend.

Crimson-colored roses bloomed through the white of Vera's blouse and flowed down the ridges and cracks of the pavers. Mimi cried and held the dying woman, looking around frantically.

"Help! Please help us!" she screamed. Over and over, Mimi raised her voice in terror and soul-crushing alarm, only to have it bounce back at her from the walls that enclosed the secluded alley.

"Mimi, stop," whispered Vera. She tried to smile but only succeeded in a death's mask grimace.

"No, no, no, no, no! You're going to be OK! I'll go find help!" stammered Mimi as the blood pooled and settled around them.

"Don't leave me, please. Don't leave me here."

Mimi sat down on the bloody pavement and gathered Vera into her arms. She rocked Vera and whispered to her, vowing to never leave her, wiping the blood from her mouth, and smoothing her glossy black hair away from her temples.

Vera's eyes closed. Still, Mimi crooned on. The police arrived and asked what happened, and still, Mimi whispered to her friend, refusing to let go of her even as the police gently but firmly lifted Mimi to her feet.

As the body of her friend, confidant, and companion was lifted into an ambulance, Mimi stumbled across Royal Street and turned onto Saint Ann, a nightmarish vision of bloody clothes and vacant eyes still whispering that she would never ever leave, never ever.

Bennette watched from the mirror as Mimi sat at her table, staring straight ahead at nothing. He had gathered enough information to find out what had happened, and his fury was immense. The one person he thought could finish this mess was dead. Her own game had finally caught up with her. The new moon was only a few days away, and given the state of Mimi, she was not going to be of any help for this moon cycle and maybe not for any at all. This unfortunate event had not been a part of his plans. While it had, of course, been a possibility given the women's choice of job and their neighborhood, he had been so focused on Vera obtaining the box that this reality had slipped past him. He briefly considered going against the elder monk's admonishments about undoing or redoing events but didn't want to face them if it went terribly wrong. It was best to wait and watch. What he would do with Mimi Blanchard, he honestly had no idea. While it was never within his plans to explicitly maintain Mimi's safety or well-being, he felt a grudging sense of responsibility given Vera's unexpected death.

He moved away from the broken woman's mirror and slipped into the quiet lavender mists of the In-Between. He needed to think. After all this time, it couldn't be a lost cause. That was unacceptable to him.

Chapter 24

Mimi stared at a space somewhere in front of her, lost in memories and visions of the past. Most were of pleasant afternoons or early evenings that she and Vera spent together—so many over the years that she was certain she could spend the rest of her life laying on her bed, smoking cigarette after cigarette, and still not remember all of them. Remembering Vera's laugh, her smile, and her fierce devotion to their friendship made Mimi's heart break into a million pieces at least a million times a day since she had stumbled home, bloody and in shock. How many days had gone by? For how many weeks had she done nothing? Surely, she must have gotten up to drink some tea or eat something, or she would have died by now, but she couldn't remember having done so and truly didn't care at all.

The sun moved across the planked wooden floors, motes of dust dancing within its rays. It should have been a cheery sight but instead added to the loneliness that Mimi felt. There was such little movement and life within the house that the dust could float about at its leisure without being blown this way or that by even the most casual shifting of the human inhabitant. And what of the non-human? The spirits of a place? Though Mimi tried with every ounce of her being to summon Vera's ghost, the air remained depressingly calm, allowing the dust to continue its sunlit pirouettes unimpeded.

She dropped her arm over the edge of the narrow, single-person bed and groped around on the floor for the pack of Chesterfield Kings. Her fingers skittered over the wood until they touched the crinkled foil of the packaging and grasped it like one would catch hold of a life raft after having been thrown overboard in violent seas.

"Dammit," Mimi glared at the crushed package. "Empty," she declared. Her voice croaked from lack of use and bounced around the empty cottage.

Sighing, she swung her legs over the side and sat up, slightly dizzy and feeling disoriented. She stood carefully and, finding herself more stable than she had thought she might be, crossed the room into the sparsely appointed kitchen where she rummaged in the cupboard for her backup stash of smokes.

"How can this be?" she whispered, finding no additional packs of her beloved vice.

Mimi looked around the room, trying to remember if she had stored the cigarettes in a different location in the kitchen, used only occasionally for preparing a meal or two, and it didn't have much more in the way of storage. The original wood stove was still there, though it hadn't been used in decades. Usually, she would eat out or enjoy hot meals at Vera's house; the memory caused her eyes to tear up. Breathing through the pain, she scanned the small kitchen. Though her memory of the last who-knows-how-long was hazy, she was certain she hadn't put additional cigarettes anywhere other than her normal home for them.

Cursing under her breath, she walked into the front room and sat at the table. The fragrant herbs planted in the cheery coffee canisters had all died, and the gas brazier within the fireplace was cold from lack of use. Counting back as best as she could, she guessed she had been in bed, smoking and dreaming, for over two weeks. Her shoulders slumped, and her chin rested on her chest as she thought about what that meant. Vera was gone. Charlie had been gone for decades now, and her Mam and siblings longer yet. She was completely alone.

The tears came hot and fast, a deluge of despair that soaked her face and ran off the tip of her nose. It was the first time Mimi had cried since Vera's murder.

She wiped her eyes and blew her nose— her tears spent. While her head ached something fierce from the rapidly released emotions, she felt more present and aware than she had in a long time. She opened the wardrobe. It was a gift years ago from Vera who thought hanging clothes on nails tacked into the plaster walls was appalling. Because Vera selected the wardrobe, it was grander than anything else in her modest cottage. She took a moment of appreciation and selected a clean blouse and skirt. Slipping out of her soiled clothes, she washed the last few weeks of confinement from her body with strong soap and cold water. After bathing, she air-dried as she gathered up the pile of clothing, stripped the bed of its sheets and quilt, and crossed to the kitchen's back door to leave the gathered clothes and bedding in the laundry tub to be washed later. If the neighbors had been watching they would have seen Mimi standing naked in her backyard, vomiting into a pile of linens at her feet. She had just come face to face with the contents of the laundry tub that was left to molder in the heavy Louisiana air during the past few weeks.

She saw the swarms of black flies first, and then the smell hit her with an unholy force that caused her to drop the soiled linens in her arms in order to cover her face against the assault.

"Oh, my god. What is it?" she moaned.

Using one hand to cover her nose and mouth, Mimi waved the fog of flies away with the other hand. As soon as the contents of the laundry tub became clear, she wished with all of her soul that she could unsee it immediately. Her clothes, once smartly tailored and respectable, were now in a pile of mildew, dried blood, and crawling insects. It must have rained at some point during her retreat from the world because an inch or more of dark brown viscous liquid covered the bottom of the metal tub. The blue cardigan with embroidered daisies was bunched and stained with gore just below the blouse it was once worn with.

"Take your sweater, Dear. It's chilly in the shade."

Mimi's stomach heaved, and she vomited repeatedly until there was nothing left. Still, her body attempted to expel the memories and the current horror in front of her.

She staggered into her kitchen, crying and scared. She had no memory of removing the bloody clothes or changing into the others. She had no memory of eating or drinking, though vomiting proved she had—and recently.

"I am losing my mind," she whispered as she washed herself once again, scrubbing her skin raw.

Mimi dressed herself and made a strong cup of peppermint tea. She found an old muslin bag that might have once carried produce inside the cupboard and, steeling herself, emptied the terrible contents of the laundry tub into it. Tomorrow the man who collected household garbage would stop by, and she would leave it for him to dispose of. She never wanted to see those clothes again.

"Take your sweater, Dear."

The kettle she had put on to boil screeched its readiness, making her jump violently. She emptied its contents into the laundry tub in the yard, swirled it around, and used a coarse bristled brush to scrub it vigorously. Once again, she was reminded that even though she was cash-heavy, her home remained years behind in modern conveniences.

"My soul for a washing machine," Mimi grumbled as she piled the soiled linens into the recently washed, sparkling metal tub and returned to the house for the next kettleful of boiling water.

The linens soaked in the tub, and the sun dropped further behind the buildings of the French Quarter. Mimi decided that it was now or never to walk to the small corner market for cigarettes, with 'never' not being an option.

"Take your sweater, Dear."

Wiping away the tear that leaked from the corner of her eye, Mimi shrugged into a beige cardigan and left her house for the first time since the only person in the world she loved had died.

Bennette watched as Mimi struggled to fully return to the present. Her self-imposed confinement seemed normal at first, but when she failed to change out of the bloody clothes, only sitting at her table staring into space, he felt concerned. On day three of this behavior, and with no water or food, his concern turned to alarm. While his head insisted that Mimi Blanchard was none of his concern, his heart said otherwise. Bennette listened to his heart for the first time in a very long time and tended to the stricken woman who was just as much a victim of the Baobhan Sidhe as her father or mother. He stripped the bloody clothing from her with no resistance and redressed her in clean attire. It felt similar to dressing a doll or a sleeping child. He brought her tea, bread, and the occasional slice of cheese which she ate with no complaint, no interest, and no acknowledgment that he was there. When he left her cottage—just a local priest caring for an ailing parishioner—she would lay in bed and smoke. He watched her through the mirror and hoped as the week progressed, she would come to, but there remained no significant change. He was both pleased and annoyed that it was the lack of additional tobacco that finally spurred her to move, but it was sorrow that flowed through him as he witnessed her full reconciliation of what had happened to Vera. Despite himself, he felt very badly for Mimi.

In the French Quarter, night gathers itself from the pavement and corners of the buildings, rising rather than falling. As the darkness rose around her, Mimi walked back to her cottage, scooting from puddle to puddle of golden gas light along the way. Her arms ached with the heaviness from the paper sacks she cradled full of coffee, sugar, laundry detergent, and cigarettes. She would have liked to have purchased some rice and bread, but she lacked the ability to carry anything else. Ideally, she would get those items tomorrow at the market stalls along the river. She might even purchase some chicken.

As Mimi imagined a home-cooked meal of vegetables and rice with boiled chicken, the clacking of the horses and automobiles faded away. So deep in thought was she that she failed to notice that another sound had materialized behind her as she continued to muddle through the ins and outs of cooking in her ill-equipped kitchen.

Clip-clop. Clip-clop.

Mimi's body reacted before her mind registered the sound, the hairs on her arms standing up painfully under the beige cardigan.

Clip-clop. Clip-clop. Clip-clop.

Mimi's heart beat quickly, and beads of sweat broke out along her forehead. She walked as fast as she could given the heavy load of groceries she carried, trying to maintain the outward appearance of a determined yet unafraid woman on her journey home. Showing fear on the dark French Quarter streets was never advisable, even if there were good reasons to be very, very afraid.

The two-footed, hooved cadence increased with her own rapid footfalls until they rang out on the pavement just behind her. Mimi glanced over her shoulder and let out the smallest of screams, her chest tight with terror. The bags of groceries dropped to the ground as her arms went limp, scattering the contents in the darkness just outside of the gas lamp's reassuring radius.

"How can this be? How can *you* be?" gasped Mimi.

The red-haired woman in a green velvet gown looked exactly as she had when Mimi first saw her thirty years ago. She also looked exactly as she had when Mimi and Vera saw her a decade after that. Her skin was flawless; no wrinkles or pox marked its alabaster color. Her lips were plump and generous pillows, stained a deep berry red. Her breasts were still high and firm under her fitted bodice and her belly still flat. The woman was stunningly beautiful apart from her eyes, green and cat-slanted. And, like a cat, her eyes showed cunning and sly amusement—a look to say the enjoyment of the hunt was just as important as the capture of the prey. Its teeth distracted from the beautiful creature with cruel eyes, warning potential prey of something exceedingly dangerous and no longer human. Its teeth were long, the canines twice as long as the rest and wickedly pointed. How it managed to close its lips around those teeth was a question for a bolder woman than Mimi. She stood, staring at the creature in horror and disbelief, stunned into immobility like a rabbit before an owl.

The Baobhan Sidhe smiled at the woman who stood paralyzed and terror-stricken before it. It captured Mimi's brown eyes in its glass-green stare and held her gaze, compelling her without words to stay still, stay compliant, to not run. After a minute, Mimi Blanchard floated away on far-off visions of picnics in the park with Vera followed by evenings playing cards beside the cheery fire in her cottage. So easily did the Fae convince Mimi to dive headlong into its glamoury of happy times that Mimi didn't feel the embrace of its arms around her body. So happily did Mimi jump at the chance to revisit her life with Vera that she never felt the deep scratches gouge her skin from hairline to collar bone. Mimi floated away from the terror of the Baobhan Sidhe and didn't realize the Fae had bent to lap up the red beads of blood that oozed from the scratches.

Mimi had roamed so far afield into her memories with Vera that when the Fae dropped her onto the pavement amidst the contents of her grocery sacks, she felt nothing. Nothing at all.

As the night retreated and gathered itself into the shadows and crevices of the landscape, Mimi was roused from her stupor by the laughing of a group of neighborhood boys who had circled her body to point, laugh, and steal her groceries. Grabbing two packages of Chesterfield Kings, she dashed down the rest of the block and threw herself into her cottage, unsure and afraid of what had happened during her walk home.

Had the ghost of Charlie Blanchard deigned to pay his daughter a visit? If so, he could have warned her. But Charlie was as neglectful in death as he was in life.

Bennette watched through the cottage's mirror as Mimi stood before it, unaware she was being observed. She ran her fingers over the burning gouges that wept blood. Four deep lines ran from her hairline just before her ear and down her neck to under her blouse's collar. She watched in horror as muddy browns, garish reds, and swirling blacks billowed up from the bloody tracks, signifying sickness, decay, and death.

Bennette stepped back from the glass and walked into the swirling lavender mists, no longer wanting to add another layer of maltreatment to Mimi's morning.

Chapter 25

As the Great Depression ran its course and the decade waned into the next, Mimi established a new sense of normalcy in her life. Without the company of her long-time companion, she no longer felt safe soliciting readings in the parks and Jackson Square. While she was an accomplished pickpocket, she had virtually given up the practice after Vera had been murdered at the hands of another thief. Seeing that violence had taken over the activity, rather than the more elegant sleight of hand that she had perfected, she preferred to err on the side of caution and keep her hands to herself.

That's not to say that Mimi was entirely without an income. While her years with Vera

had been happy, fulfilling, and lucrative, she
was still a product of her environment and
remained tenacious, street smart, and adept at
thinking outside the box. These skills landed
her in a small tearoom on Chartres Street
where she was hired as a tea leaf reader. It
had never occurred to Mimi to go legit. In
fact, she didn't realize it was even an option.
However, wandering aimlessly one afternoon,
she passed the small storefront with its
discreet hand-lettered sign that simply
announced *READERS WANTED*. She ducked
inside and was greeted by a charming café
with scattered tables and chairs populated by
women in the most fashionable clothes who
sipped tea from delicate porcelain cups. A
lady with an elaborate rolled hairstyle
finished her tea, placed the empty cup onto its
saucer, and waited. As Mimi watched the café
and its customers, a gentleman in a jaunty
bow tie walked over and took a seat across
from the lady who had just finished her cup of

tea. He placed the saucer on top of the cup, quickly flipped them both upside down, and reset the saucer on the table, the cup now empty and placed off to the side. As Mimi watched this performance, colors began to swim around their heads. Bright greens and vibrant pinks danced about the coiffed head of the woman. Bubbles of silver bloomed and popped within the pink streaks like the effervescent soft drinks that had become even more popular once they were freed from soda fountains and available for purchase in shimmering glass bottles at any market.

Around his head, the man had gentle, rolling waves of dark blue with an occasional crest of frothy dark green, all comforting and calm but with a depth of emotion below the surface of the blue waves. Mimi concentrated and made out splashes of burgundy and purple below the dark blue's undulating surface. The soft-souled man had suffered violence in his past but never repaid in kind. A gentleman, indeed.

Mimi was so lost in her own reading of the reader and his client that she jumped when the woman let out a jubilant laugh, clutching both hands against her still-flat stomach.

"A little girl?" she trilled, smiling broadly.

"Yes, ma'am. A little girl," confirmed the reader with a soft smile.

Mimi smiled with them both, gladdened by the good news. Suddenly, there was a flash of red that only she could see, and she heard the deep Italian voice of one of the spirits from her tarot cards.

"This will not go well for the lady. The baby is not her husband's child."

Mimi stood mute. She didn't have her cards with her; how were the spirits talking?

"Ah, it's true," came the sing-song lilt of the Haitian spirit. *"The lady will not live to see the girl-child. Her lover's wife will raise it as her own."*

The delicate French of the hanged woman concluded the tragic tale, *"All planned, all planned. The wife could not conceive. The paramour could, so, voila! A family made."*

"That can't be right! The reader would have seen this!" Mimi replied in her thoughts to her attending spirits.

"The reader is limited by his view of the symbols on the plate. He will not open himself to the realm where true communication is found. Symbols are a gateway; the man remains in front of a closed door," sighed the hanged lady as blues washed through the reader's aura.

"But he is capable. I can see that myself!" thought Mimi in response to the French lady, spinning endlessly from her noose.

"It is not safe for him to see true, or so he believes. Great punishments have been visited upon him in the past, and now he only sees the symbols," reported the Italian.

"But I 'see true,' as you say, and I have had many punishments and tragedies in my past," protested Mimi.

"Ah, for you, Pitit Mwen, it is dangerous not to," crooned the fierce Haitian.

Mimi watched crestfallen as the perfectly dressed young woman paid the reader and exited the tearoom with nothing but happiness and joy shining through her aura. Maybe the reader, even if he was ignorant of the truth of the situation, had provided her a blessing.

"May I help you?"

Mimi turned toward the voice. It came from a woman a little younger than herself who stood smiling and waiting to seat her at a table.

"I've come about for the job as a reader," she replied, matching the hostess's smile as her spirits showed her showers of money.

Mimi had found a location that provided her with a safe place to continue work. While she wouldn't use her tarot deck for readings any longer, her spirits let her know that its symbols were only one of many ways to access their wisdom and advice; spent tea leaves could be used just as easily.

After a brief chat with the owner, Mimi secured her position, gladly taking the normally unwanted afternoon shift that gave her a less fearsome walk back to her cottage before the streets fell dark. She would begin the following week, and it was suggested she visit a salon on Canal for a more updated hairstyle and maybe a smarter suit or two. Mimi thought how happy Vera would be with

a shopping trip and smiled sadly as she left
the Bottom of the Cup and walked up to
Canal Street in search of a hairdresser.

Chapter 26

Bennette watched Mimi's return to the outside world with interest. It had taken her a couple of years, but by 1936, she had established herself as a sought-after reader at the tearoom. With the extra income, she managed to add several modern conveniences to her Saint Ann Street cottage. Bennette doubted Mimi would have ever bothered doing so if Vara's more luxuriously appointed town home had remained available to her. However, once the floodgates opened, so to speak, it seemed Mimi truly enjoyed a home that provided both shelter and ease of living. The old wood stove in the kitchen had been replaced with a more modern gas range and running water and indoor plumbing followed shortly thereafter. Bennette, despite his insistence on staying removed and neutral regarding Mimi Blanchard, was pleased to see she had put together a life for herself.

Bennette's observations of Mimi's world weren't limited to her successes; the monk knew she was the last direct link to the Baobhan Sidhe, and he knew the Fae had been stalking Mimi since shortly after Vera had died. Some of the attacks Mimi remembered in great detail while others stayed with her as vague dreams or memories of something not quite right, but the details proved insubstantial.

Over time, Bennette had noticed a pattern, cruel in its efficiency. The Fae's physical attacks of feeding upon Mimi were spread out, allowing the vicious gouges to heal before it attacked again. This allowed the Fae to stalk its prey slowly, its strength maintained, to prolong the hunt and amusement for the predator. The Baobhan Sidhe was, above all else, a clever predator, and it was having an enormous amount of fun preying on Mimi Blanchard. After a while, it was clear that another aspect of the Fae's attack was the psychological toll that chipped away at Mimi. The physical attacks were occasionally remembered, but between one horrific feeding to the next were the tortuously vague incidents of stalking. Mimi would turn a street corner and catch sight of the Fae, but with a second look, it would be gone. Had she really seen it? Walking alone in the French Quarter, Mimi heard the sound of two hooves matching her own footfalls, coming closer and closer as the Fae gained ground on her. When she spun around, nothing was behind her at all. Had she really heard it? Night after night, dreams of Vera's blood being lapped up from the pavement by the red-haired Vampire dragged her from sleep with a heart-wrenching scream, leaving her exhausted but too afraid to return to bed. Finally, the Fae would act, drinking her blood and thus restarting the cycle. How the woman endured was beyond Bennette's ken.

Despite his powers of observation provided by navigating the openings within different times and places from the In-Between, Bennette had still not devised a plan to deal with the Fae's box. He desperately wanted to skip the process of going through the seemingly infinite probabilities that would lead him to his desired outcome and simply do the chore himself, but the warnings of centuries of elders held him fast. He found it beyond frustrating that, in Mimi's time, the odds of reaching his desired outcome were convoluted and tangled due to the sheer number of humans the Fae interacted with.

"No! This can't be!" Bennette shouted as he watched in amazed frustration. A gaggle of novice nuns moved back and forth in front of the mirror he favored at Charity Hospital. Its position at the landing of the third-floor staircase provided him the best vantage point to see who came and went from the large attic space where the Fae's box was stored. Each young nun carried armloads of linens, boxes, and bags down the stairs, down the hallway, and out of view of his mirror. A more senior nun stood watch, reminding the younger Sisters that the space needed to be cleared quickly or it would all become rubble once the structure was torn down come Monday.

"Let's move, Sisters! We must make haste! Whatever is not needed for the new hospital will be sold and the funds used for additional necessities. Sister Mary Theresa! Have you not been listening? Nothing can be reused or sold if it's left in the building! Why are you dilly-dallying so?"

Bennette maintained his gaze on the young nun called Sister Mary Theresa who, indeed, was not listening to the older nun. Sister Mary Theresa was fortunate that her elder was unable to see she was staring into the mirror at the landing. The cornette that covered her head obscured her face from the side. Staring into mirrors would be frowned upon, much more so than dilly-dallying.

Whichever infraction she might be accused of, Sister Mary Theresa was certain that it would not be listening to a monk speaking to her through a mirror. She wondered if she was hallucinating, but she thought it was more likely the monk in the mirror was a spirit. Her training had attempted to dispel the superstitions and beliefs taught to her by her mother and grandmother, but the young woman learned early on in her tutelage to say what was expected and keep quiet of the rest. To her mind, dismissing the existence and messages of spirits was just as dangerous as refusing to acknowledge the blaring horn of an automobile one had stepped in front of.

Bennette had found a nun with the Sight.

"Aye, Sister. The box is small, the size of a loaf of bread, with a hinged lid. It is hidden on the floor just above us. When you locate it, you must destroy it," Bennette explained. The intensity of his instructions was born from the new knowledge that the hospital would be torn down Monday. There was no more time to wait for a moon phase to bring the Fae back to its de facto home turf.

The young woman listened and nodded. Curiosity bubbled in her mind, but to question a spirit was dangerous. Best to do what the man in the mirror asked and send him on his way.

"I understand. I will look under the furthest windows. Perhaps it has been hidden there. When I locate it, shall I open it?" she whispered.

"No! Do not open it. Remove and destroy it, and then forget we had ever spoken."

Bennette watched as the young Sister turned and ran up the steps to the third floor, just one more in a long line of young women climbing and descending the steep stairs leading to the old building's attic.

Sister Mary Theresa moved to the farthest reaches of the gabled attic. She thought if the box was hidden so long ago, it must have been before the attic had filled to nearly overflowing. She walked past ancient wheelchairs, broken crutches, a box of carved wooden legs and feet, and trunks of bedding and sheets packed with camphor. Floor lamps, metal tables on wheels, desks, and doors of all conceivable shapes and sizes littered the space. If there had been a rhyme or reason to the packing or placement of the attic's items, it was no longer evident.

Trying to not look as if she was wandering aimlessly—after all, there were many eyes who would file a report if one didn't pull their own weight—the Sister picked up a small box of patient files dated from before she was born and walked around searching for the hidden box. As she made her way around a large floor fan with half of the blades missing, she stifled a cry of relief. Resting against the base of the fan was a wooden carton that held a variety of household and kitchen items. Mary Theresa looked around to make sure she was not being watched then knelt in front of the carton. Just visible below the layer of spoons, pads of paper, stained linen napkins, and various cookbooks was an ancient wooden box the size of a loaf of bread. She carried the carton and made her way back, through the piles of clutter, to the stairs and down to the next level. Walking past the mirror, she noticed it only reflected the hallway; the monk was gone.

"The spirit knows that I did as asked," she whispered in satisfaction. It was always lucky to have a spirit that was happy with you, and the young nun was pleased to complete the task he asked of her.

"What's in here, then?" the grounds keeper asked gruffly as Sister Mary Theresa held the carton out to him.

"This and that, some old spoons, moldy cookbooks, rotten linen."

"Over there," he spat. His annoyance with the whole process was evident to anyone unlucky enough to approach him. The old man thought this entire chore was unnecessary. Anything that was in the attic space hadn't been used or even thought about for at least fifty years. Best to leave it to the demolition crew.

Sister Mary Theresa walked in the direction indicated by the old man lifting his chin. She handed the carton to a younger man who, while not as angry as the groundskeeper, wasn't exactly chatty.

"I was told to give this to you," she said in as neutral a voice as possible. Sounding excited about garbage would raise suspicions, but she was excited. A spirit had spoken to her, given her a task, and she had accomplished it! She couldn't wait to tell her grandmother about this extraordinary afternoon the next time they had a visit.

The young man took the carton from her, swiveled in one smooth motion, and heaved it onto the truck that was piled high with other bits of discarded refuse. By the time the sun set, the pile would be reduced to ashes, burned into oblivion.

Sister Mary Theresa walked back to the old Charity Hospital building. She found it hard to believe that this time next week, the hospital would be gone. A new, modern hospital would be nice, but the loss of this one still stung a bit.

"Oh! Excuse me, sir. I'm so sorry!" she stammered and blushed behind her unwieldy headpiece. Lost in thought and not paying attention, she ran directly into a man pulling a wagon full of antiques that had been removed from the attic, destined to be sold in the high-end shops around the city.

"Pay it no mind, Sister! No mind at all!" smiled the man, flush from thinking of all the new inventory he would surely make a good profit from.

The antique dealer moved along his way, and the novice nun moved on to her mid-day supper as the preparations for the demolition of Charity Hospital continued at a steady pace.

Bennette slid down the trunk of his favorite oak tree and watched the mists swirl their lilac and lavender hues, changeable yet constant.

He felt tired but content. Finally, the box had been found and would soon be burned, destroying the refuge of the Baobhan Sidhe. He prayed it was enough. His head slid off to the side as his breathing slowed, and he dreamed of his beloved Aisla.

"I did it, Aisla. I did it..."

Martin Dupree heaved the wagon full of assorted knickknacks from Charity Hospital's attic over the bumpy and uneven pavement to his new antique shop. He was beyond thrilled to be one of the few people permitted to acquire a wagonload of items to sell on behalf of the Sisters. He would be able to purchase more inventory with his cut of the sales, allowing him to establish his store much faster than he had at first imagined.

As he unlocked the door and pulled the heavy wagon into the empty shop, he couldn't help but grin widely. His father had sneered at his idea for an antique store and argued it would never survive. Just wait until he paid his son a visit next week and saw the shelves displaying the beautiful and unique items he had acquired.

Martin switched on the fan that sat on the counter, flipped on the lights, and got to work. He unpacked several sets of china, tea sets, and one beautiful gravy boat that went with nothing else but was too pretty not to price and set out for sale. The next carton contained small porcelain boxes with the names of various herbs and spices painted on them. They were certainly pretty but were missing the shelf on which they must have originally sat.

"No matter," smiled Martin, rubbing years of dust and grime from each one. "You're all so pretty that I'm sure you'll sell just as you are!"

Martin often spoke to items as if they were people because, to him, each cup, saucer, knife, fork, and castaway book had its own personality. He loved them all and saw his shop as an adoption center of sorts.

He displayed the spice containers on the shelf closest to the door and turned to the wagon once again. The final box contained miscellaneous flatware that would be the easiest to display. After a quick rinse of warm water and vigorous rub with a clean rag, all were placed in a beautiful basket to sell individually. That only left the pile of heavy drapes at the very bottom of the wagon. Martin hadn't particularly wanted the drapes, but the older nun who oversaw the process of clearing the attic had made it clear that you took whatever she gave you, and that was that.

Sighing, Martin lifted each panel out of the wagon to shake out the copious amount of wrinkles and dust.

"Well, you are actually quite attractive, aren't you?" he whispered to the yellow-washed silk panel. The stitched lining added a great amount of weight to the panel and doubtlessly helped block the vicious rays of the subtropical sun.

Dust and more than a few dead beetles dropped from the folds of the second panel as Martin shook it free from its wadded-up siblings and spread it gently across the counter, smoothing the wrinkled silk and crooning endearments to it. Satisfied that the second panel was in good shape, he reached for the third. As he lifted the heavy fabric from the wagon, an unexpected clatter and crash made him jump, and he dropped the curtain at his feet. He stepped around it to inspect what caused the commotion and saw a perfectly nondescript wooden box on the shop floor. It was about the size of a small loaf of bread, and its slightly rounded lid was hinged.

"Well, what do we have here? A stowaway, perhaps?" Martin asked the box as he bent to pick it up.

"Hmm. You're still quite handsome if not just a tad plain, eh? No matter, someone will see you and love you. I'll make sure of it!"

He set the box aside and added it to the list of things that needed to be polished, repaired, or unlocked. He would likely display it with the hand tools later, but for now, Martin was busy addressing the appalling wrinkles on the last panel of silk. He assured the final panel that he would straighten them all out and provide the perfect home for it and its sister panels.

Chapter 27

With the Great Depression over and the war years bringing a measure of comparable prosperity, Mimi had been busier than ever at the Bottom of the Cup. Her small group of regular customers had tripled in number and, adding them to the steady stream of walk-ins made her afternoon work hours often spread well into the evening. The money was good, and although Vera had been gone for many years now, Mimi still missed her terribly. The long hours at work kept her from being alone at home. She had been on a few dates here and there over the years, but she would inevitably slip up and alienate people by forgetting to properly hide her abilities, mentioning situations or events that she had not been told about. The requests for a dinner or stroll dried up. It was painfully apparent to Mimi that she could not be herself with the people who asked her out, so she stopped making herself available. She would rather grow accustomed to her own company than be continually hurt by others not wanting it. Still, she was lonesome and gladly took on the longer shifts to fill up her hours before bed.

Bed. She began each day by looking forward to getting back into bed. It seemed she could never get quite enough sleep. Nightmares plagued her, and she often awoke in a panic, certain she had heard the sounds of hooves walking about her cottage. Try as she might, the strangely amorphous night-time hours were never clear enough to analyze what exactly was going on. She even tried speaking aloud to herself in an attempt to recreate a conversation with another person, but that only resulted in her feeling foolish;

the activity added no additional insight or clarity. Mimi found herself sinking into a resigned acceptance. What she couldn't change or understand, she allowed to carry her along like a rogue leaf in a stream. This habit, born from the trauma of her childhood, continued to function as her backup response no matter how far she pulled herself from the life of that hungry and dirty street child. It was a trait she shared with her own mother, herself a victim of the Fae's follies.

Feeling her knees click as she stretched, Mimi looked around the tearoom and checked out the ladies who stopped in only to enjoy a day out and some tea and the others who came in specifically for a reading. Today, they were split about half and half in the dining room. Rarely was there a day where no one wanted a reading, especially since Mimi had come on board. Her reputation as a thoughtful and astonishingly accurate reader gained steadily. Now, several years after her start, it was nearly impossible to sit with her without an appointment. Clients remained boggled that she could receive so much information from the mess of wet plant material she tipped onto the saucer. When asked, Mimi simply smiled and talked about what she saw. Revealing that spirits spoke to her would have frightened the majority of her clients, resulting in the loss of her much-valued income.

Watching the colors dance and waver above the heads of the tearoom's visitors, Mimi stepped over to the counter and poured herself a glass of sweet tea. Hot tea had its place, but her mid-afternoon pick-me-up was the cold variety. Lighting a cigarette, she scanned the room at her leisure, enjoying the small break in her packed day.

Had her beloved Vera stepped into the tearoom, she may not have recognized Mimi Blanchard. Upon her acceptance as a reader, she took the comment made by the manager to smarten up her appearance to heart and spent several days doing just that. Now, her hair was most often done in one version or another of a Victory Roll, and her suits were tailored of the finest fabrics with military-sharp shoulder pads and skirts with a single kick pleat in the back. The woman who worked in the women's clothing department was forever trying to get Mimi to try softer-looking dresses or even a bolero-style jacket, but Mimi preferred the power-suit silhouette. Not only did she feel strong, but its severity was an armor that screamed 'stand back!' to anyone who might decide to be too friendly or forward. Despite her dramatic outward transformation, she was still devastatingly practical. She wore lace-up spectators that made walking home on the uneven pavements of the French Quarter easy. To fall and break an ankle wouldn't serve at all, so she didn't chance it with delicate-heeled pumps. All in all, Mimi's new look was of a strong woman not to be trifled with—a look that served her well.

Bennette watched the ebb and flow of people walking in and around Jackson Square. He had taken a risk to step into Mimi's time. Having found a set of robes more modern and discreet than his brown wool, he remained largely unnoticed—just one of many clergymen who worked in the large church.

The 1940s made him nervous with its frantic pace and large numbers of people. Try as he might, he had been unable to convince himself that the young nun had found and destroyed the correct box, so his presence in this time was required. The attacks against Mimi continued, and the Baobhan Sidhe had not assumed the body of another human, meaning the original box that contained the monster's homeland soil still remained. Bennette desperately wanted to believe the Fae had been destroyed. He had almost convinced himself that Mimi's scratches were from her insistence on wearing wool suits and her nightmares born from a life of assorted tragedies and difficulties. It was only when the Fae became brazen enough to enter Mimi's cottage, pacing and grinning as its prey lay in a fitful sleep, that Bennette allowed the truth to settle like a dead weight on his heart; the Baobhan Sidhe lived. Extensive time spent meditating and ruminating on the situation had left him with no viable options but to come to Mimi's time. He would need to see first-hand what the Fae was doing and locate the box himself. Though the elders of his own time had adamantly opposed his direct involvement, Bennette's fears outweighed their warnings. He feared if he didn't stop the Fae soon, he would never

have the chance again, and the death of his
Aisla could never be avenged.

Mimi crossed Jackson Square, her sensible
heels clicking against the pavement. The sun
was setting, and the shadows crawled up
from the corners of the buildings. Crossing
the square was a populated shortcut back to
her street. She actively tried to avoid being
out alone after sunset, and since she was
almost always alone, she was rarely out past
dusk. Her memory had grown too foggy and
her fatigue too great for her to feel strong
enough to fight off any danger should it
approach.

The glare of the setting sun made her turn
her face to the more shadowed front of the
enormous, spired structure, and she found
herself making direct eye contact with a lone
priest standing on the steps.

"Father," said Mimi with a proper nod of her head.

Clergy of any kind made her nervous because she was certain they would see her as a non-attending heathen. But Catholic clergy made her especially nervous. Her family had always been Catholic, but she had never—not once—attended mass. Her Mam was too ill, and Charlie was too drunk or altogether absent to consider the spiritual well-being of their children. Considering she barely had enough food to eat or shoes to wear, sending Mimi to church would have been a strange way to decide to be a parent. But in this predominantly Catholic city, Mimi was intensely aware that she was a non-involved parishioner. Given her unconventional job and her history of outright thievery, she thought her chances of entering the beautiful church without incurring a strike of divine lightening were slim to none.

Bennette watched as Mimi Blanchard walked quickly past him, giving him the most cursory of greetings then ducking her head to avoid any further eye contact. How angry would she feel if she knew he had been watching her for her entire life? How irate would she be if she knew he was aware of the creature that had orphaned her, and that he had been unable to stop it?

"I'll find the box, Mimi. I'll find the box, you'll be safe, and my Aisla will rest."

Bennette was surprised that seeing Mimi in person reignited his desire to stop the Fae. He stepped onto the pavement and walked into the small alley that led him to Royal Street. He imagined that Vera's blood still stained the flagstones, but it was only the shadows that rose with the setting sun.

Chapter 28

That night, Mimi dreamed she was being smothered, gauzy wisps over her face and invading her nose. Try as she might, she was unable to move her arms to free her face from the hated material. Or was it a spider web?

"Oh, god," she moaned in her half-aware state, "not spiders. Please, not spiders…"

She drifted off into a strange, floaty place, not awake yet not asleep, a perpetual nowhere free of concrete thought and awareness. When she gained back her awareness, she had no idea how long it had been and struggled to wipe the smothering material from her face again. This cycle would repeat throughout the night until sunlight finally roused her from her struggle. She was left feeling exhausted, fuzzy-brained, and sick to her stomach.

"What is happening to me?" Mimi asked herself as she stood in front of the mirror, gazing at the image of a woman who looked at least a decade older than herself.

Her skin was sallow, her eyes ringed with dark smudges, and her hair was brittle and lackluster. The wounds along her neck had almost healed. Mimi remained strangely unconcerned about the recurring channels gouged in her skin every few weeks.

"It must be part of the Fae's glamoury," whispered Bennette as he stood on the other side of the mirror, watching Mimi take stock of herself.

"There is still so much I don't know about this fiend," he sighed and stepped away from the mirror as Mimi, on her side, began her morning toilette.

Bennette was single-minded, at times cold, and not altogether friendly, but he did try to respect basic rules of decorum. Besides, he had not yet located the Fae's box. Based on Mimi's deteriorating condition, he didn't have much time left. Soon enough, the Baobhan Sidhe would either kill her outright and move on—meaning he would lose track of the creature—or take her over completely, and he would have lost yet another human to the monster.

Mimi gulped her morning tea, selected her clothing for the day, and rolled her hair, attiring herself in what she had started to consider her work uniform. As tired as she was, she had a full day of readings scheduled.

Bennette had his own work scheduled for the day. He stepped out of his preferred mirror—one that hung in the darkened hallway of a seldom-used wing in St. Louis Cathedral—and made his way out into Jackson Square. He thought about the irony of his situation; he had acquired the skills to move into and out of times and places and had learned that time and place were, in essence, relative to the person experiencing it. Still, he remained stuck in the construct of linear reality, choosing the times and places that immediately served his needs. Soon, he suspected, he would need to step ahead of the current situation, but the warnings of his elders remained burned into his spirit, and he continued to exercise caution.

"Not that it seems to help at all," he muttered as he made his way around a group of sightseers and cut through the alley to Royal Street.

"The probabilities that reach the desired outcome are much more tangled now. I doubt even the Ancient Ones could have seen how many people have become part of this tale, each adding to the probabilities and roads that may or may not result in my success."

Bennette maintained his philosophical grumblings as he avoided groups of tourists and wandering locals. After a brief walk, he arrived at the block that housed the lower-end stores that carried items resembling cast-offs and curiosities more than valuable antiques. After scouring every high-end antique store on Royal Street, he hadn't seen anything that remotely resembled the Fae's box. If he failed to locate it somewhere on these next few blocks, he honestly was unsure how to proceed. He couldn't peer through every mirror in New Orleans in the hopes that this small, nondescript wooden vessel would happen to be sitting within view. The probability of destroying the Baobhan Sidhe was quickly becoming unattainable.

For the next several hours, Bennette browsed the various shelves and cabinets full of knick-knacks and outright junk in shop after shop. He found dull knives and shears, chipped pottery, cracked porcelain, gorgeous crystal, and cheap glass baubles, but there were no plain wooden boxes. Oh, there were boxes, to be sure—there were boxes woven of rushes and reeds, music boxes, ceramic boxes to hold ladies' gloves, and some wooden boxes, but none were plain. Inlays, paintings, and carvings adorned all the wooden boxes the despondent monk had located so far.

Hours passed, and still, Bennette had not located the box. By late afternoon, hunger and thirst demanded that he stop his search and attend to his still-human body. The rich, savory scent of pork led Bennette around the corner to a food cart selling meat pies and wrapped sandwiches on loaves of bread as long as his arm. As hungry as he was, he doubted he could eat one of the massive sandwiches himself and ordered a meat pie.

Bennette carried the pastry to a bench that was enough out of the way to avoid the large groups of pedestrians and sat down in the shade to watch the throngs of people and enjoy, as best he could, his solitary meal.

Around the corner and out of Bennette's sight, Martin Dupree's door opened, knocking the bell attached to it and singing the arrival of a customer.

"Good day, sir! Welcome, welcome!"

Martin's natural enthusiasm was apparent in all of his interactions, and it rarely failed to elicit the same good humor in his customers. This was not one of those times.

The man who walked through Martin's shop doors was tall and imposing—large in the way of a boxer or bullfighter. His hair was a dark mahogany that shone red in a certain light, and his skin was so tanned it resembled shoe leather. He wore all black and western-style boots that rang out dully on the shop's wooden floor. The man's largeness was not just physical; he had a presence that filled the room, allowing no one else in the space the benefit of perceived privacy. He smiled widely at Martin, but the smile never reached his eyes.

Martin was not comfortable at all, a feeling that was quite extraordinary for him, and he retreated behind his counter, allowing the imposing man to roam the shop at will.

After what seemed an eternity, the man dressed in black stopped in front of the plain wooden box, now polished to a mellow sheen, from the old Charity Hospital. He cocked his head, listening to a whisper that Martin couldn't hear. While intensely curious about what the man was listening to, Martin found himself happy he could not hear what his customer could.

Nodding slightly, the large man brought the box to the counter.

"Is there a key for this box?" the customer's voice rumbled and reverberated about the small space, making Martin's teeth grit and his eyes water.

"No, sir. It arrived without a key. I can pry it open for you, though, if you'd like. I believe something is inside it," Martin said as slowly as to control the wobble and waver of his voice. The man's presence was almost more than he could take.

"No, do not open it. I'm sure I have a key that will fit this lock. I'll need this wrapped well; I'm traveling."

Martin nodded his head rapidly, took the cash offered by the customer, and stuffed it into the register, not bothering to count it. He wanted this strange person out of his antique shop so he could close early for the day and calm his nerves with a nice glass of wine. Later, he would discover that the man in black had paid him more than double what the price on the box requested.

"Certainly. My pleasure," whispered Martin, his heart running at double-time in his chest. "Where will you be traveling to, sir?" he asked timidly as he handed the securely wrapped parcel over the counter.

Tucking the bundle under one arm, the man walked away. Martin thought he had heard him say '*Horton Bay*,' but the sound of the bell as he opened the door to leave left the frightened shopkeeper unsure. Perhaps he had heard correctly. But truly, as long as the man was gone, Martin didn't really care where Horton Bay was. It was not here, in New Orleans, and that's all that mattered.

Martin walked quickly to the front door, flipped his open sign to closed, and turned off the lights. He was closing early for the first time since he had opened the business and didn't care one bit. All he cared about now was a glass of red wine in his comfortable chair safe at home, his cat on his lap and the strange man far, far away.

Chapter 29

Mimi woke up cold and wet, her back sore from the hard pavement and her stockings ripped to shreds. Her neck burned as if a hot poker had been pressed against her skin, and her mouth felt like she had been sucking on a cotton ball for the last week.

Gingerly, she sat up. Her vision swimming, she scooted to the curb, hugging her knees and rocking back and forth. She was so sick.

Passers-by saw the middle-aged woman sitting on the curb, rocking, and talking to herself, and they gave her a wide berth. Whether drunk or mentally ill, it was all the same in the French Quarter. Don't make eye contact, and don't speak to the unfortunates who lived on the streets.

Mimi's soft moans turned to loud cackles as a young man dropped a dollar bill in her lap, never breaking his stride or looking at her directly.

"Oh, my god. I've become Charlie!" she laughed and cried.

If only she could remember what had happened and why it continued. Had she taken up drinking without knowing it, or had she simply gone crazy?

Pulling herself to a standing position, Mimi smoothed her wrecked skirt over her destroyed stockings in a pitiful display of lady-like manners. She looked around to see where exactly she was. After identifying the closest landmarks, she realized she was blocks away from both her work and her home.

Judging by her clothes, she had left one without making it to the other.

Mimi hitched her breath in against the rising hysteria that bubbled up from her chest and stepped gingerly across the street and down the road that skirted the edge of the French Quarter furthest from the river. This would take her to her street without having to go directly through the neighborhood that had been home her whole life. She couldn't bear to be seen in her current state.

The sound started shortly before she turned onto Saint Ann Street.

Clip-clop.

Clip-clop.

Mimi froze. Her body responded as any prey would—rapid heartbeat, shallow breathing, and muscles tensed to run. Her brain? Her brain remained confused and fuddled. What was that sound? Why was it so familiar?

Clip-clop.

Clip-clop.

"Hey, lady! You sure look rough! Hard night?"

The rude words and loud laughter cut through Mimi's foggy thoughts, and she turned to see who was laughing at her.

A single man leaned against the building to her right. Or, at least, he might be a man if a man could have the face of a reptile. The lizard-like man grinned, displaying razor-sharp teeth, and its forked tongue flicked in and out of the lipless mouth obscenely.

Mimi didn't bother to hide that she could see what the man truly looked like. She was exhausted, sick, and terrified. The lizard-man was the final straw; Mimi Blanchard screamed. As her scream expelled itself from her throat, her muscles took note and propelled her forward. She ran faster than she thought possible, screaming, laughing, and crying. Passengers in passing automobiles watched the poor woman in shabby clothes running down the street, hysterical laughter bubbling out of her like poisonous lava, and commented to their companions about the ills of drink.

Mimi turned the corner onto her street, slowed to a limping walk, and stumbled into her cottage.

The sun was high and bright, and she vaguely thought she was going to be late for work. Swallowing another bout of hysterical laughter, she kicked off her scuffed shoes, tore her ruined clothes from her body, and padded, naked, into her bathroom. Cranking the water to its hottest point, she stoppered the tub and stood there, letting the steam obscure her vision. Years ago, when she had finally saved enough to have the bathroom added to the back of her cottage, she had thought it was the pinnacle of her achievements—a testament to how far she had made it away from life with Charlie. Now? Now she stood here naked, alone, afraid, and filthy from a night spent sleeping on the street. As she sank into the scalding water, Mimi sobbed. She would never be anything more than the insane daughter of an insane drunk.

"Oh, my head..." Mimi moaned and sat up in bed. Her head pounded, and her eyes were dry and gritty like someone had violently rubbed sand into each one and taped them shut for the night.

She threw the heavy quilts off of her then, shivering, grabbed them back and wrapped herself up.

"Naked. Why am I naked?" Her voice bounced around the empty space.

Wrapping a robe around her shoulders, Mimi put a kettle on for tea and sat at her table, trying to piece together what had happened that left her clothes in a ruined heap on the bathroom floor and her naked in bed.

The kettle screeched. Mimi shook her head, instantly regretting it, and stood to prepare her tea. Over the years, she had collected proper cups, saucers, plates, and cutlery, but her first few items, stolen so long ago, remained her heart's joy. She smiled into the homely little mug as the steam of chamomile and mint tea bathed her sore eyes and cleared her head. The first sip was a balm, and she thought she might just make it through the day after all.

"What day is it?" Mimi felt the spinning of disorientation creep back and threaten to overtake her as she realized she had absolutely no idea what day it was. "How long have I been in bed?"

Cinching her robe more securely around her thin frame, she opened the front door a small crack and peeked outside. Bags of rubbish lined the curbs; the garbage collector hadn't been around yet, so it was Thursday.

"Can't be. I couldn't have laid in bed for two days!"

Mimi walked back to her bed and sat down, feet swinging and toes dusting the wooden planks of the floor. Her mind was a whirlwind of what she remembered or what she might have dreamed. It was all so foggy that it was impossible to decipher reality from sleep images. She decided that her bath must have been true since she woke up in bed with no nightclothes on. But what of the rest? The lizard-man? She hadn't seen those strange creatures in years. Was her recent memory of them something that was real, or had she dreamed it?

After finishing her tea, she rolled each shoulder to release the tension and winced. The wounds on her neck burned. How had she been injured? Why couldn't she remember?

The beautiful redhead watched Mimi through the slats of her louvered front door. The creature was torn between two overwhelming desires. Should it continue to play with its prey, enjoying the human's confusion and fear so much like her mother before her, or occupy the body now as the box that provided a refuge was traveling far away from the French Quarter?

The Baobhan Sidhe smiled slyly. Either decision was delightful as each had its own amusements inherent within. Its cat-green eyes slanted in concentration. The human body it occupied was growing old and had become starkly thin. Perhaps it had played too long with it. Having a human host was fun, but having a human body that expired without the box nearby could be troublesome. The monster grinned, its pointed teeth pressing against its full lower lips.

"Ah, Miriam, daughter of Mary, you'll be sent to rest soon enough. Soon enough," the Fae chuckled with cruel mirth as it stepped away from Mimi's door. The creature had decided the woman's fate as one would decide to put a horse to pasture.

Clip-clop.

Clip-clop.

Clip-clop.

Mimi froze, her leg partially in her trousers. She was not going into work. She felt ill, weak, and had no explanation prepared for her absence. As such, she would wear her comfortable slacks rather than her rigid suits that were her public armor. For now, she would stay home and be as comfortable as possible until she could decide what she would tell her bosses at the tearoom.

The noise came again, like mules clattering along, pulling their carriages. But this sound reflected only two hooves, not four. Flashes of Charlie trying to explain to her his panic and confusion pulsed past Mimi's closed eyes as her heart beat painfully against her ribs.

Clip-clop.

Clip-clop.

The sound moved away from the house, becoming more indistinct. Mimi's heart settled a bit.

"Charlie, why are you everywhere right now?"

Mimi didn't expect an answer. She wasn't adept at seeing human ghosts, and if she were, she still doubted the shattered spirit of Charlie Blanchard was roaming the French Quarter. And yet, all of the terror and confusion of the last year mirrored Charlie's last few months. Why?

Trying to understand the questions about why and how exhausted her. Laying back on the bed and watching the sun move across the room, Mimi dozed off. Once again, she found herself caught in the gauzy tendrils of half-remembered dreams and long-past events. Though she was dangerously depleted and desperately needed sleep to heal, it evaded her still.

402

Chapter 30

As Mimi's mental and physical wellbeing continued to deteriorate, Bennette's concern grew, and his hunt for the Fae's wooden box became more desperate, to no avail.

Mimi couldn't take her thoughts off Charlie. As her mental health spiraled downward, her acknowledgment of their shared experiences morphed into the delusion that he had never actually died and that, maybe, he was stalking her now. Paranoia wrapped itself around Mimi Blanchard like a rotten and moth-eaten shawl.

"You son of a bitch! You may have taken some things from me, but you'll never get it all!" Mimi muttered as she skittered around her cottage, gathering her most precious possessions. She collected the green glass drinking cup, her silver knife and fork, and a few pieces of faded Blue Willow china. Mimi—a wraith that spoke to a man long-dead and secreted her valuables in a hole in the floor of her house—no longer resembled the street-smart con artist that Vera loved or the power-suited, accomplished reader employed at a trendy tearoom. This woman was ill in body and mind and had long ago fled rational thought.

Bennette watched what remained of Mimi and cried; he had done this. His refusal to act directly had doomed the daughter of Mary, who had been doomed herself when the demon fled his Aisla. All innocents. All of them. Except, perhaps, the cook whose pettiness and greed had started this whole disaster. Bennette barked an ugly laugh devoid of humor. He had no idea what had become of that wretched woman.

"Aye, I hope she choked on any good fortune that the beastly Fae granted her," he hissed as he watched Mimi pace in circles around her cottage muttering and gesticulating to the ghosts of her past.

The sun moved past its zenith, and Mimi left her house. Reality broke through her delusions on occasion—most often when her body demanded food, drink, or in this case, cigarettes.

As she made her way to the corner market, mumbling and whispering to herself—just another demented character inhabiting the French Quarter—Mimi heard it. Like a jolt of electricity that cleared away the tendrils of madness wrapped around her, she found herself clear-headed for the first time in a very long time.

Clip-clop.

Clip-clop.

Clip-clop.

Mimi's eyes were as large as saucers, her breathing painfully rapid, but her mind was as clear as it was going to get. That sound meant danger, and it had since she was a small child. She spun around and saw the stunning redheaded woman walking toward her.

Clip-clop.

Clip-clop.

Clip-clop.

She watched in amazement as the creature grinned at her, exposing viciously long teeth, and walked right past her.

Mimi blinked. What was happening? Why did it simply walk by?

Despite her fear, she began walking, keeping pace with the monster that had been a part of her entire life. Mimi had no doubt that it knew she would follow, but why?

The Baobhan Sidhe turned the corner, and Mimi scurried after it, winded and tired but determined to see what the monster was up to.

Further ahead, at the entrance to the corner market, which was Mimi's original destination, stood a small child. She was a toddler just past infancy. Her hair was the red of a burnished penny, and she glowed. Mimi had never seen anyone shine as bright as this little girl. She watched the cars go by, looking over her shoulder at the door to the market every few seconds. Mimi assumed the little girl's mother had slipped in for a loaf of bread or an onion; perhaps she would bring her daughter a small bit of candy for waiting outside so patiently.

As Mimi watched, the little one stepped to the side of the building where a shiny square of metal was hung. At one point in its history, it had been a sign advertising tins of crackers, but the sun and the pounding rains had reduced it to its original sheet metal, now shining brightly in the late afternoon sun. The little girl smiled at her reflection and waved, delighted to be able to see herself without standing on a chair or stool like at home.

The Baobhan Sidhe stopped, considered the small child in front of it, and nodded its head—a decision was made. Mimi's blood felt like ice as the Fae turned to look at her, acknowledging that Mimi had indeed followed, and winked.

"NOOOOO!" Mimi's scream came out as a cracked and croaking screech so full of horror that Bennette was pulled from his meditations in the In-Between.

Following the woman's pleas and cries, Bennette ran through the lavender mists finally locating a place to see Mimi, watching in horror as the blood-drinking Fae bent over a small child standing outside the corner market.

Mimi launched herself at the green velvet-clad monster, putting herself between it and the little girl who fell backward out of the way. Years of physical and emotional abuse by the Baobhan Sidhe, however, had taken their toll. Mimi was weak and easily winded; the Fae was not, and it was very angry at being pushed aside from its new host. Bennette watched in horror as the Fae leaned over Mimi, crumpled on the pavement. In flashes of horror, Bennette saw the monster grin, its teeth as sharp as daggers. It leaned over Mimi and caught her gaze as easily as a snake would grab the gaze of a squirrel. The creature's talon-like nails delicately skipped down Mimi's skin from her hairline to her shoulder, again and again until Mimi's blood ran in rivers onto the dirty sidewalk. Bennette was caught in the terror of the moment and couldn't help but notice the similarity to Vera's death. Suddenly, the screams from the little girl wrenched him from his morbid revelry; the Fae was standing and walked toward the child, grinning in anticipation.

Clip-clop.

Clip-clop.

Clip-clop.

Bennette knew what the monster intended and simply could not allow it to take the child. Whether it meant the Baobhan Sidhe would die without a host or go to ground within its box that had yet to be located, he didn't know. However, he was absolutely sure that his time to manipulate the situation from afar was over. Bennette stepped out of the mirrored sheet metal, snatched the child, and hauled it back into the In-Between. The shriek of the Baobhan Sidhe sent the crows scattering and crying wildly as its future host was ripped from its grip. It turned to Mimi who it had left bleeding on the pavement, but the body was already growing cold.

Bennette clutched the terrified child and watched as the Fae spun on its hooves and winked out of view, presumably in search of the box. Bennette dearly hoped that the Fae's refuge had somehow been destroyed and that it would soon die like a plant unable to sink roots into the soil.

Stepping back from the opening, the monk considered the child in his arms. He could put her back just as he found her, except for Mimi's dead body that was still on the ground and the unknown whereabouts of the Baobhan Sidhe that may still come back and take her as its host. Considering the Light that shone so brightly about the child, Bennette had no doubt that the Fae would easily find her, and he refused to allow it.

Singing softly to the toddler, Bennette watched as she slipped into sleep. Her shock was winning against the desire to stay awake and see where she was and why the fog was purple. He walked along a road conjured by his desire to see the child to safety until he heard the song of a great body of water.

Adjusting the sleeping child in his arms, he stepped in front of a mirror framed in simple pine and gazed through; it was a one-room rectory of a church, and it was empty. While he couldn't tell which time the room existed in, he could tell the apartment was safe. Bennette quickly stepped through and looked around. Catholic. He smiled; this would work. Laying the sleeping child on a settee positioned under the window, he looked around the simple apartment until he found paper and a pencil and began to write. When he finished, he laid a crocheted afghan over the tiny girl and sang softly, opening her and allowing her gifts to flow freely. He had a feeling she would be needing them. Bennette left the note on the pillow next to the toddler's head, kissed her cheek, and stepped back into the mirror. He would need to attend to Mimi now.

Shortly after Bennette made his exit, a small, rounded belly man with a cleric's collar bustled into the rectory with an armload of pamphlets. He stopped in surprise at the sight of the little girl fast asleep on his sofa.

"Her name is Ashlynne, and she needs a home," the befuddled priest read aloud from the note Bennette had left with the child.

The toddler woke up and began to cry, and the priest called out for his secretary. He had no idea what to do with a homeless child that appeared like magic in his front room.

From outside the window, a large owl that blinked its cold eyes at the bright light that shone from the red-haired girl watched as the priest and his secretary bustled about the apartment. Satisfied, the massive bird took flight, soaring high over the blue waters of Lake Michigan.

Chapter 31

Mimi sat on her bed, her knees pulled up under her chin and her arms wrapped around her legs. Her house looked the same, but the air seemed smoky. She couldn't remember how she got there.

"Mimi."

The voice was gentle, and yet Mimi found that it made her feel sad.

"Mimi, you need to look at me."

Mimi looked up and gasped as a man gazed out at her from her mirror. He smiled and then, grasping the edges of the frame, pulled himself up and stepped out, landing with a thud on the wood floor.

Mimi thought she should be much more concerned by this than she was, but everything seemed strangely blunted. There were no sharp edges to her environment or her emotions.

"Who are you?" Mimi's voice sounded raspy and hollow to her ears.

"My name is Bennette. I've come to help you."

"Are you a spirit?" asked Mimi in a whisper.

Bennette smiled sadly, "*I'm* not the spirit, Miriam."

He watched her as incomprehension gave way to incredulity—all of it written upon her face like a movie marquee.

"No, I can't be a spirit! That would mean I'm dead. And, obviously, I am not!" declared

Mimi, waving her arm around the room as proof of her aliveness.

"Oh, aye? You think because you are in your own home that you are alive?"

"Well, yes. If I were dead, wouldn't I be somewhere else? I mean, not *here*?"

"Sometimes people go *somewhere else,* as you say. Sometimes they don't know to do so, and they go where they are safe. As you have," he finished softly.

Mimi looked around her house. It looked like she was gazing through a film of smoke or haze. In her heart, she knew what Bennette said was true, but she didn't want to be dead. She didn't want to leave this world just yet.

"You don't have to, you know," said Bennette.

"Don't have to what?"

"Leave. You can stay and watch. You can even watch different times and places. Whenever you're ready to move on, it's easy enough."

Mimi sat and stared into the smoky haze for a long while, Bennette waiting patiently.

"What happened to the little girl?" she finally asked as the events that proceeded her death finally caught up to her.

"She's safe. I saw to it myself," replied Bennette.

"And the monster? What of it?"

"I don't know. If you choose to stay for a bit, I will tell you all about it."

"And if I don't?" countered Mimi, eying the monk suspiciously.

"Then the knowledge will have no benefit for you."

Mimi sat while Bennette watched. After a moment, though time had stopped meaning much to Mimi, she smiled sadly at Bennette.

"I would like to stay awhile. I would like to know about the monster that killed my family and me."

Bennette held out his hand, and Mimi stood. Grasping his hand, she allowed herself to be led through the glass where mists of purple and lavender swirled around her head and caressed her cheek.

"Where shall I start, Mimi?" Bennette said, dropped her hand, and smiled.

"From the beginning, I imagine," decided Mimi as she struck a match against Bennette's oak tree, lit her cigarette, and inhaled deeply.

Bennette smiled as she blew three perfectly round smoke rings above her head.

"Aye. In the beginning, there was a young man who loved a beautiful girl," began Bennette, starting with the only beginning that truly mattered to him.

The End

April 24, 2022

East Jordan, MI